"I do not intend to be a part-time father,"

Harrison said, "which leaves us only one alternative."

"Which is?"

"That Georgia has two parents."

A frown creased Kimberley's forehead. "But how—?"

"There's only one way." He said it without expression. "That you marry me."

Kimberley stared at him. "You cannot be serious."

"Oh, but that's where you're wrong, Kimberley." He smiled. "I am. Deadly serious."

SHARON KENDRICK was born in West London and has had *heaps* of jobs, which include photography, nursing, driving an ambulance across the Australian desert and cooking her way around Europe in a converted double-decker bus! Without a doubt, writing is the best job she has ever had and when she's not dreaming up new heroes—some of whom are based on her doctor husband—she likes cooking, reading, theater, drinking wine, listening to American West Coast music and talking to her two children, Celia and Patrick.

SHARON KENDRICK

Part-Time Father

Harlequin Books

TORONTO • NEW YORK • LONDON
AMSTERDAM • PARIS • SYDNEY • HAMBURG
STOCKHOLM • ATHENS • TOKYO • MILAN
MADRID • WARSAW • BUDAPEST • AUCKLAND

This book is dedicated to the beautiful and talented
Daniella Trendell.

ISBN 0-373-11820-1

PART-TIME FATHER

First North American Publication 1996.

Copyright © 1995 by Sharon Kendrick.

This edition published by arrangement with Harlequin Books S.A.

® and ™ are trademarks of the publisher. Trademarks indicated with
® are registered in the United States Patent and Trademark Office, the
Canadian Trade Marks Office and in other countries.

Printed in U.S.A.

CHAPTER ONE

'MOTHER! *Mother*!' Out of breath from running at top speed up the path following her mother's urgent summons, Kimberley dropped her suitcase on to the cold tiles of the flagged floor and listened.

Silence.

Fear gripped at her heart like a vice, and a note of uncertainty crept into her voice. 'Mother?'

She heard the scrape of something in the small sitting-room, and, striding over in the shortest time possible, she threw open the door to see her mother just moving the small stool which stood in front of the sofa, on which she'd obviously been resting her feet.

Thank heavens! The unacknowledged fear, ever present when your elderly mother lived on her own, immediately subsided. 'So *there* you are!' said Kimberley in relief.

Her mother pushed her spectacles further back up on her nose and looked at her only child, a small smile lighting her still shapely mouth which was so like her daughter's. 'Where did you think I'd be?' she enquired mildly. 'Robbed and left trussed up in the attic? Kidnapped by modern-day pirates and heading for the coast?'

Kimberley giggled. 'You *are* outrageous, Mother! Your imagination is much too vivid, and those crazy adventure stories you read don't help.'

5

'And you don't read enough of them!' commented Mrs Ryan sternly. 'You're far too serious about that job of yours.'

Kimberley decided to ignore that—for who wouldn't be obsessively career-minded when their love-life was a total non-starter? And whose fault is *that*? mocked a tiny inner voice.

Ignoring that too, she went over to plant a kiss on her mother's forehead, then perched on the other end of the sofa. 'Why did you need to see me? I was coming down soon for Christmas anyway. You are OK, aren't you? What are you doing lying down in the middle of the day?' And then her attention was caught by the bandage which was tightly tied around her mother's ankle. 'Oh, heavens— whatever have you *done*?' she exclaimed in horror.

'Kimberley, please,' said her mother calmly. 'There's absolutely no need to panic.'

'But what have you *done*?'

'I've sprained my ankle, that's all.'

'But what does the doctor——?'

'He says it's *fine*, I just need to take it easy, that's all...' Mrs Ryan's voice tailed off. 'The only problem is——'

'What?'

'That I can't work.' Mrs Ryan leaned back against the cushions piled on the sofa and surveyed the immaculately dressed form of her daughter, who was at that moment letting a frown mar her exceptionally pretty features.

Kimberley gave a little click of disapproval. 'Then give the job up, Mum,' she urged. 'I've told you that I earn enough to send you what Mrs

Nash——' she said the name reluctantly '—pays you.'

'And I have told you on countless occasions that I enjoy the independence which my little job gives me, and I have no intention of relinquishing it.'

'But, Mum—must you do a *cleaning* job?'

'You, Kimberley, I'm ashamed to say, are a snob,' said Mrs Ryan reprovingly.

'I am *not* a snob. I'd just rather you didn't work at all, if you must know.'

'You mean,' said Mrs Ryan shrewdly, 'that you'd rather I didn't work in the big house which you almost became mistress of?'

Kimberley's mouth tightened, but she felt tiny beads of sweat break out on her forehead. 'That's history,' she croaked.

'You're right. It is. In fact, I've some news for you.'

'What kind of news?'

'He's getting married. He's engaged!'

The beads of sweat became droplets. Kimberley heard her heart pounding in her ears, felt the blood drain from her face. 'He is?' she croaked, dry-mouthed. 'That's wonderful.'

'Isn't it? Dear Duncan,' said her mother fondly.

'Duncan?' asked Kimberley weakly.

Her mother gave her a strange look. 'Yes, of course Duncan. Your ex-fiancé, the man you were going to marry—who else could I have meant?'

Surreptitiously Kimberley wiped the back of her hand over her sticky forehead, and then, terrified that her mother might notice and comment on her pale complexion, searched around for a distraction. 'How about some tea? I'm absolutely parched. Shall I make some?' she asked brightly.

'Best offer I've had all day!'

Kimberley quickly left the room and filled the old-fashioned kettle with shaking hands, re-acquainting herself with her mother's tiny kitchen, pulling biscuits out of the tin with trembling hands as she tried to put her thoughts in order. She wondered what her mother would have said if she'd known that Duncan had been the last person in her thoughts; she had thought she'd been talking about Harrison.

Harrison Nash—her ex-fiancé's brother. The man with the cold grey eyes and the hard, handsome features and the lean, sexy body. Harrison Nash—who had changed the whole course of Kimberley's life without even realising that he was doing so...

It had been one bright and beautiful summer's evening, with the setting sun pouring like golden honey into the red drawing-room at Brockbank House where Kimberley had been waiting to conduct what was obviously going to be a difficult and painful interview with Duncan, her fiancé. Because, after much thought and many sleepless nights, Kimberley had decided to break off the engagement which had followed their whirlwind romance.

Duncan and his mother had recently moved into Woolton village's most imposing building—the historic Brockbank House, left to the Nash family by a distant relative who had died without leaving an heir. Kimberley had met Duncan when she'd been visiting her mother in the village, on one of her brief but regular forays from London, where she lived.

From the first meeting he had pursued her avidly, and, flattered by his charm and his persistence, Kimberley had allowed herself to believe that she had fallen in love at long last. Already in a strong and powerful position at work, where her male colleagues tended to fear and revere her, Kimberley had been charmed by Duncan's healthy irreverence and his ready agreement to let *her* set the pace physically.

He didn't leap on her and he respected her somewhat old-fashioned view that she wanted to wait until they were married before consummating their relationship. At twenty-four she thought that she'd found the perfect gentleman—and she *had*.

Kimberley sighed.

It just wasn't *enough*. Quite apart from the fact that she was three years older than Duncan, and that he was still at university while she had already established a successful career for herself in London, there was one even more important reason why she could not marry him.

She simply didn't love him—or rather, she did, as the dear, sweet person he was, but not in the way that he said he loved her, and to marry him under those conditions would simply not be fair to him.

She had decided to tell him as gently as possible, but Duncan was young, good-looking and the best fun in the world. He would get over it, of that she was certain.

Kimberley sighed as she perched nervously on the edge of one of the large chairs in the red drawing-room, brushing one hand through the thick abundance of raven-black hair and pushing it off her high-browed face so that it spilled in shiny soot-dark waves down her back.

She wondered how one went about breaking off an engagement. She would have to tell her mother and Duncan's mother—both widows. She herself had no other relatives, and Duncan very few. She wondered briefly whether the older brother in America had been informed—the rich, successful one, who Duncan and his mother both seemed slightly in awe of.

Probably not. They'd only become engaged last weekend—hardly time to make it properly official.

As Kimberley stared out of the window at the magnificent grounds of Brockbank House she heard a soft noise behind her. Not a footstep exactly, it was much too subtle for that, but she suddenly experienced the unease of being watched. She turned round slowly, to discover who her silent scrutineer was, feeling her skin ice with some unknown fear as she stared at the dark, silent man who stood before her.

She had seen photos of him before, of course—various portraits of him scattered around the house and, latterly, newspaper clippings from gossip columns—but Kimberley would have known without being told that this was Harrison. Harrison the rich, the powerful, the blessed older son. Not that he looked in the least bit like Duncan, although the familial similarities were there.

But this man was Duncan's very antithesis. Where Duncan's eyes were soft, smiling, this man's were hard and crystalline and bright. Where Duncan's mouth was full and kissable, this man's lips were a thin, hard line. Cruel lips, thought Kimberley wildly, and tried but failed to imagine them kissing her, her cheeks flaring red as she saw those same lips twist into a contemptuous curve.

For one frozen moment Kimberley sat staring up at him, unable to move, to think, to speak, unable to do anything other than acknowledge the dark and potent and sensual rush of desire which flooded over her with the heavy pull of a tidal wave. She stared into eyes which no longer looked grey but black as the night, she saw the heated flare of colour which scorched along his high, perfectly chiselled cheekbones—and she felt dizzy with a shameful longing.

Unnerved by that still intense scrutiny, and by his silence, Kimberley scrambled to her feet.

'You must be Harrison,' she blurted out, in nothing even resembling her usual calm, confident manner.

'And you must be the fortune-hunter,' he observed caustically, withering contempt written all over his face.

For a moment Kimberley thought that she must have misheard him; it was just not the sort of thing which one expected to hear, certainly not in civilised company, but there again, with that raw, scornful censure blazing from those amazing eyes, this man didn't look in the least bit civilised. He looked . . .

Kimberley shuddered.

Almost *barbaric*.

She forced herself to remain calm, because some instinct told her that if she responded on his level she would live to regret it. She raised her eyebrows fractionally. '*What* did you just say?' she queried, quite calmly.

'Oh, dear,' he said mockingly, and sighed. 'I should have guessed that it was too good to be true—you couldn't possibly have brains as well as beauty. I called you a fortune-hunter, my dear. It's an old-fashioned term, whose meaning is quite simple——'

'I'm well aware of what it means,' Kimberley cut in, but her voice was shaking with rage, and deep within her a seed of hostility blossomed into rampant life. 'How dare you?'

He shrugged his broad shoulders. 'Quite easily. You see, you might find this peculiar, but I happen to be rather protective of my kid brother. And what else am I supposed to think when I hear that he's about to marry someone he hardly knows, who happens to be years older——?'

'Only three,' she interrupted furiously. 'And what difference does that make? Lots of men marry women older than them.'

'Do they?' His look was cool, assessing. 'And do lots of older women marry inexperienced college-boys, who stand to gain huge inheritances? Is that what turns them on—*Kimberley*?'

She shivered with some dark nebulous recognition as he said her name, the way his tongue curved round it making the very act of speaking into the most sensual act she had ever encountered.

'I don't have to stay here and listen to this,' she said shakily, but her feet were rooted to the priceless Persian carpet and she was incapable of movement as she gazed into mesmeric grey eyes.

'But stay you will,' he ordered silkily. 'And listen.'

She watched, horrified, as his eyes dropped to her body and lingered insolently on the lushness of her breasts beneath the thin cotton T-shirt she wore, and Kimberley was powerless to stop what that appraising stare was doing to her.

She felt a dart of something which was a combination of pain and acute pleasure, felt her breasts grow heavy, hard, swollen. She saw his mouth twist with derision as he observed the blatant tightening of her nipples, and at that moment she felt utterly cheap.

He nodded his head, as though satisfied by something. 'Yes,' he said thoughtfully. 'As I imagined. A hot little body and a face like a madonna—quite exquisite, but unfortunately they are such ephemeral assets. And, wisely, you've decided to capitalise on them. But I'd prefer you to do that with someone other than my brother. Understand?'

Kimberley bit back her rage, her normally sharp mind in dazed turmoil because he was still staring at her breasts, and her nipples were torturing her with their exquisite need to have him take each one into his mouth, to suckle slowly and lick and...

Horrified, she stared back at him, her body's appalling reaction to his scrutiny stinging her into defending herself. 'I don't have to capitalise on any assets I might have, actually,' she retorted. 'Because I happen to have a very successful career in a merchant bank.'

'And how did you get it?' he queried insultingly. 'On your back?'

His hostility rode every other thought out of her mind. 'Why are you doing this?' she whispered incredulously.

He shrugged. 'I told you. I'm looking out for my brother—and he needs shielding from women like you.'

'Women like you'.

Her face flaming, Kimberley lifted her hand and slapped him hard—very hard—around the face. She should have been shocked at her violent reaction but she wasn't; it was the most satisfying thing she had ever done in her life. But he didn't flinch. Only the angry spark which glittered ominously from the grey eyes betrayed his emotions.

'In a minute,' he said calmly, 'I shall respond to that. But first I want you to listen very carefully to what I'm going to tell you.'

'I don't have to listen to anything you tell me. You insulting——'

'Spare me your misplaced anger and shut up, *Kimberley*,' he said in a voice soft with menace, and Kimberley felt a shiver ice its way down the entire length of her spine. 'My brother is on the threshold of his life. Emotionally he is immature. If he marries now it will be a huge mistake. He is not ready for marriage.'

And neither was she, though Harrison Nash did not know that. She saw the grim determination on his face, the arrogance and the dominance. A man used to getting his way at all costs. How far, she wondered, would he go to prevent her from marrying Duncan?

And Kimberley suddenly knew an overwhelming and very basic urge to get her own back for his insults, for that sexual scrutiny which had had her responding in a way which sickened her.

All at once she was filled with the most tremendous exhilaration, exultant with the sense of her own power to anger this man. 'You can't stop us marrying!' she told him coolly.

The grey eyes narrowed calculatingly as he registered her change of mood. 'No, you're quite right. I can't.' And here he paused, so that there was a brooding, forbidding silence before he resumed speaking. 'But what I *can* do is to withhold any of the financial hand-outs from my company to which Duncan has quickly become accustomed. This house is legally mine, although I have always intended to transfer the deeds to my mother and Duncan, since I have enough homes of my own. However, I *could* change my mind...' He gave her a questioning look. 'I imagine that Duncan's attraction might wane if he didn't come with all the trappings you'd expected?'

Kimberley had met many cynical, ruthless men during her years in the City, but this one, this dark and cruel stranger, made the others look like amateurs.

She lifted her head proudly. 'If I wanted to marry Duncan, then nothing *you* could say or do would stop me,' she said truthfully. 'So you've lost, haven't you?'

'I never lose, Kimberley,' he contradicted her softly. 'Never.'

She fixed him with a look of mock-polite disbelief, fascinated in spite of herself to know just how far he would go to achieve what he wanted. 'Oh, really?'

'I have a proposition to put to you.'

'Go on,' she said, very quietly.

He spoke with a certain reluctance. 'I'm prepared,' he said heavily, 'to offer you a financial incentive of your own if you agree to call the wedding off. If, on the other hand, you refuse and the wedding goes ahead, then I'm warning you that you will receive nothing from Duncan's inheritance unless I am satisfied that the marriage is a good one, and one with solid foundations. Do you understand?'

The grey eyes were so hard and so cold, making a mockery of the rugged perfection of his features, and another shiver of apprehension sent icy claws scrabbling all over Kimberley's skin. 'It isn't just because I'm older, is it?' she whispered, shaken by his venom, her desire for revenge for his insults momentarily forgotten. 'Or even because you think that I'm marrying Duncan for his money? You really don't *like* me, do you?'

He went perfectly still, so still that he might have been carved from some unforgiving stone. 'No,' he said eventually. 'I don't think I *do* like you, if liking can be gauged after such a short acquaintanceship, but you are correct in your assumption in one way—your age and your greed are not the real reasons why I want you to call the wedding off.'

'Why, then?'

'It's simple. Because you are not the right woman for him.'

Stunned by the sheer unremitting force with which he spoke, Kimberley stared into his hard, cruel face. 'What on earth gives you the right to say that?' she whispered.

'This does,' he said, in a voice which was brutal with some unnamed emotion, and he caught her by the waist and bent his dark, savage face to kiss her.

Something happened to her—something irrevocable and mind-blowing. Something which was to change her life forever. What the hell had he done to her with just one kiss? she wondered desperately. Because sexual desire, fiery and hot and potent as life itself, began blazing its way through her veins as his mouth found hers.

Oh, God, but it was heaven.

Heaven.

She opened her mouth to him as though she had waited all her life for that sweet, punishing kiss. She found herself trembling, almost swaying, now wanting more, much more than his kiss. She wanted him to touch her where no man had ever touched her; she wanted those long fingers to remove her T-shirt, to kick away her jeans. She wanted him to lay her down on the floor and make love to her right there . . .

But then reality crashed in with a sickening sensation as, distantly, somewhere in the house, she heard the sound of someone shouting. She felt his hands drop from her waist, felt, too, his tongue withdraw from her mouth, where it had been inciting her with provocative little movements which had mimicked what no man had ever done to her.

She gave a kind of automatic protest as he lifted his head up and stared down at her dazed face, and she read the contemptuous look in his eyes.

'I rest my case,' he said insultingly.

Kimberley straightened her spine and stared back at him, hiding her shame behind the frosty glitter in her blue eyes.

In her eyes sparked the hatred she felt for him. To illustrate his point he had treated her no better than a whore, and in a way she had responded no better than a whore. The way she had felt in his arms had frightened her with its intensity, so that all her carefully fought for self-control had vanished like the wind. She was the vanquished, he the victor. He had all the power, and she had none. And she never wanted to see him again, not as long as she lived.

Never.

But then Kimberley discovered something else. She could see that behind the contempt which distorted the angular features there remained a hunger—a savage, sexual hunger which made his eyes glitter blackly and beat a frantic pulse at the base of his neck. He wants me, she thought, yet he despises me. And he's a man who gets exactly what he wants.

Oh, my God, thought Kimberley weakly. He'll come and find me. And what if I can't—what if I just *can't* resist him? What will a man who despises me offer other than instant heartbreak?

Unless she somehow contrived to make him despise her so much that he'd leave her alone forever.

She gave a small, smug half-smile, and allowed the kind of cold, calculating look which she knew he would be expecting to come into her eyes.

'This—er—financial incentive you're offering,' she purred. 'How much are we actually talking about?'

Some light in his eyes died. If she had thought she'd read scorn and derision there before, it was nothing to the look which now replaced it. He looked at her as though her very presence contaminated the air surrounding him.

He mentioned a sum, and she allowed a rapacious little smile to curve her lips upwards as she nodded. 'I'll do it,' she told him. 'On one condition.'

He shook his head, the contempt hardening his mouth into an unforgiving line. 'No conditions, sweetheart,' he drawled coldly. 'Unless I make them.'

- She shook her head. 'I won't do it unless you agree not to tell Duncan *anything* about what's happened here this afternoon. I want to tell him— to break things off—in my own way.'

He stared at her incredulously. 'Do you really think I'd hurt my brother like that? And, much though I'm tempted to tell him about his lucky escape, I'm really not cruel enough to disillusion him with the knowledge that he fell in love with a cheap little tramp. Do I make myself clear?'

'Perfectly.' She held out a slim white hand, which was miraculously free from tremor. 'And now, if we can conclude our *business*.'

She saw his barely concealed shudder of distaste as he took a cheque-book out from the inside pocket of his suit and began to write.

What she hadn't expected was that it should hurt quite so much...

Kimberley raked her hand roughly through her hair, as if the frantic movement could somehow magically dispel the image of Harrison which burned on her mind's eye as if it had been branded there. After more than two years, she thought despairingly, it shouldn't be quite so vivid. She wasn't naïve enough to have expected to forget a man like Harrison Nash, but surely by now just the merest thought of him shouldn't be enough to make the heat rise up in her blood with its slow, insistent throb?

She picked the tea-tray up to carry it back through into the sitting-room where her mother was waiting.

Why remember all that now?

Because she remembered it every time she came home; it was one of the reasons why her visits were more infrequent than either she or her mother liked. This place was tainted with memories of Harrison Nash and that one fateful kiss.

The day after he had kissed her she had done several things. Firstly, and most importantly, she had gone to Duncan and gently given him back his ring. He had not railed or argued with her; he had quietly accepted her stumbling explanation, saying that deep in his heart he had not been completely surprised.

The following day Kimberley had fled to stay with an aunt in Scotland, where she had remained for a fortnight, quietly licking her wounds. She had also cashed the cheque which Harrison had given her and given the money to charity. More importantly, as she'd handed the huge wad of money over to the bemused representative of Save the Children, she had made a solemn vow. That she would put Harrison Nash out of her mind forever.

And so far, at least, it hadn't worked.

'Kimberley!' came her mother's voice. 'Where's this cup of tea you promised me?'

'Just coming!' Fixing a smile on to her face, Kimberley took the tray and biscuits in, and poured out two cups.

The Earl Grey tea was deliciously refreshing, but Kimberley, though hungry, took only one bite out of a biscuit then left it—still ruffled about remembering that extraordinary day.

Forcing her mind back on to safer subjects, she offered the plate of biscuits to her mother. 'How are you going to manage with your foot bandaged?'

'Oh, I expect I'll be all right,' her mother replied unconvincingly.

Kimberley hid a smile. Her mother, love her, was like an open book! 'Would you like me to come and stay with you until you're up on your feet properly again?' she asked.

Mrs Ryan's smile could have lit up Oxford Street. 'Oh, *would* you, dear? I'd be so grateful!'

Kimberley's mind skipped along. She could telephone her bank later. She was a conscientious high-flyer in the merchant bank where she'd worked for the past five years—she doubted whether they'd mind her taking a break at such short notice. 'Of course I don't mind,' she said. 'But I'll have to drive back up to town to get some clothes.'

'That's fine, dear,' said her mother contentedly as she eyed the teapot. 'Is there another cup in the pot?'

Kimberley poured her mother another cup. 'So, who's Duncan marrying?' she asked, glad that the boy she'd been so fond of had found someone else to love.

'Some girl he met in America—an heiress, apparently.'

'That will please Harrison,' commented Kimberley acidly.

Her mother gave her a shrewd look. 'I don't know why you won't hear a good word said about that man. He's actually very charming.'

'Charming?' About as charming as a snake-pit! Kimberley gave a forced little laugh. 'That's the last adjective I'd use about *him*!'

'But why do you dislike him so much?'

'How can I dislike him—I've barely met the man?' said Kimberley dismissively, then relented. 'If you must know he stands for everything I hate— all that arrogance! He thinks he's God's gift to women——'

'A lot of women tend to agree with him,' cut in Mrs Ryan in amusement. 'Or so I'm told.'

Kimberley resisted the temptation to scream. 'I'd better leave now,' she said hurriedly, in order to stop her mother from regaling her with any anecdotes about Harrison's life. 'If I set off now, I can be in London and back before dark.'

Her mother frowned. 'Well, do drive carefully, won't you, dear?'

'Don't I always?'

'Do you? You're a little too fond of the accelerator, in my opinion!'

But Kimberley was a good, careful driver—though she *was* slightly on the fast side. She made good time to London, and just over an hour later her scarlet sports car drew up outside her delightful honeysuckle-covered cottage in Hampstead.

She phoned her office and spoke to her boss, who told her to take as long as she liked off work.

'Seriously, James?' she laughed.

'No! Take all that back—I'll miss you too much!'

'I'll call you when I get back—I should only be a few days!'

'Call me sooner, if you like. That's if you need a broad, manly shoulder to lean on.'

'I'll bear that in mind, James,' said Kimberley, before ringing off.

James had never made any secret of his admiration for her, but he was confident and rich and handsome enough not to take her laughing refusals to go out on dates with him to heart. She had told him she never dated people she worked with, which was true. Although she actually had a reason for not dating *anyone* who happened to ask her.

She had tried dating, and it didn't work. She couldn't cope with the physical thing. The unfortunate legacy of her brief kiss with Harrison was that no other man moved her in any way that even remotely resembled the way she'd behaved in his arms that day.

Which was a good thing, she reasoned, since she had been so disgusted with herself afterwards. If passion turned you into a wild, mindless creature at the total mercy of your body—then you could keep it! Kimberley would manage just fine with her brain!

She emptied her fridge, cancelled the milk and switched on the answerphone, threw her suitcase into the back of her MG, and set off back up the motorway.

Her journey was uneventful, save for the episode when a low, black and infinitely more powerful car than her own forced her to move over into the middle lane and then roared off spectacularly into the distance. For Kimberley, who took some pride in her driving and was fiercely competitive, this proved irritating.

Obviously a man, she thought, slightly unfairly. Probably someone who's into phallic symbols to compensate for his own weediness.

She saw the car again, parked outside the one really up-market restaurant in the village, which was a few miles from her mother's house and well off the beaten track—not a tourist trap at all. And she wondered vaguely who, round here, was driving such an expensive piece of equipment.

She arrived back at her mother's, unpacked and then concocted some supper from the food she'd brought with her. The two women were just enjoying a quiet glass of wine when Mrs Ryan dropped her bombshell.

'Er—Kimberley?'

How well she recognised that voice! Kimberley felt a bubble of amusement welling up inside her. 'Mother?'

'I'd like to ask you a favour, dear.'

'I somehow thought that you might. Go on—ask away.'

'Er—it's a little difficult to know how to put it.'

Obviously a very *big* favour, thought Kimberley. 'Mmm?'

'You know I mentioned that Duncan's got engaged?'

Kimberley smiled. Mothers could be so transparent! 'Yes, Mum—and I don't mind, honestly!'

Mrs Ryan gave her a severe look. 'I wasn't imagining for one minute that you did—since you were the one to break it off. Still, better before the marriage than after, I always say.'

Kimberley sighed. 'You were saying?'

'Oh, yes. Well, the thing is that he's due to arrive in a couple of days' time and, with my leg and all, there's no one to get the place ready for him...'

Kimberley put her wine-glass down on the table and looked incredulously at her mother. 'I'm not sure what you're getting at, exactly.'

'Well, I was wondering if you could help me out?'

'Help you out?'

'Just stand in for me—until my leg is better.'

'You mean—*clean* Brockbank House for you?'

'That's right, dear.'

Kimberley shook her head. 'I'll pay someone from the village to stand in for you.'

Mrs Ryan shook her head. 'But I doubt you'd get anyone at this short notice, and so near to Christmas. Besides, you know how fussy Margaret Nash is—she won't let just anyone near all those antiques.' She caught a glimpse of her daughter's expression. 'You wouldn't have to do much, darling,' she said hastily. 'Just hoover the place and flick a duster around. And the kitchen floor could probably do with a bit of a wash. I mean——' she gave Kimberley another stern look '—look on it as a kind of atonement, if you like.'

Kimberley blinked in astonishment. '*Atonement*?'

'Mmm. It would be rather a nice gesture, wouldn't it—after jilting Duncan? Getting the house nice for him. Unless, of course, you're not being entirely truthful with me. Perhaps you *are* a tiny bit jealous . . .?'

Kimberley stared at her mother very hard, before throwing her head back and laughing loudly. 'You know, Mum, for sheer cheek you're world-class!' Then she thought of something else. 'But surely Mrs Nash wouldn't want me near the place?'

'Oh, no, dear—she's quite happy to have you there. She likes you, you know—she always has. She always said that she thought you were quite wrong for Duncan.'

Interesting. She hadn't said a thing at the time. 'Oh, did she?'

'Will you do it, then?'

Kimberley sighed. 'I suppose so! Anything for a quiet life. But only on one condition.'

'Yes, dear?'

'Where's—Harrison?'

'Oh, he's in France or Germany or somewhere. Living there while he takes over another company. His mother says he works himself into the ground. She says——'

'Fascinating as I'm sure you and Mrs Nash find it,' Kimberley interrupted coolly, 'I really have absolutely *no* interest in hearing about Harrison.'

Her mother's face said, Well, you did ask me!— but to her eternal credit she didn't utter another word.

It was just unfortunate that hearing about him was one thing, but trying not to think about him was another—and the moment she set foot over the threshold of Brockbank House more memories of that hateful, scheming man came flooding back to haunt her.

Kimberley wondered how she could have allowed herself to be talked into doing this particularly distorted 'favour' for her mother. She hadn't been near the house, not for over two years, not since that dreadful day when Harrison had given her the cheque.

Despite her mother's assurances she had been dreading seeing Mrs Nash, but Duncan's mother held her hand out immediately she opened the front door. She was a tall, graceful woman, with Duncan's soft brown eyes; Harrison, Kimberley knew, was the image of his father who had been killed in a yachting accident when both boys were quite small.

'Hello, Kimberley,' said Mrs Nash. 'It's good of you to help me out.'

'It's no trouble. Really. Mother insisted I stand in for her.'

Mrs Nash smiled. 'Eleanor's so terribly conscientious. I really don't know what I'd do without her.' There was a pause. 'She told you that Duncan's getting married?'

'Yes, she did.' Kimberley hesitated. 'I'm very happy for him, Mrs Nash. Really, I am.'

Mrs Nash smiled. 'I rather thought you might be.' She laid her hand on Kimberley's arm. 'Won't you come and have some tea with me?'

Kimberley shook her head. 'Another time, perhaps. I'd rather get started, if you don't mind.'

'I understand.'

Did she? thought Kimberley. Not really. She imagined that even the fairly liberal Mrs Nash would be shocked if she knew the real reason for Kimberley's reluctance to linger any longer at Brockbank House than she needed to. What would she say if Kimberley told her that the sight of that framed silver photograph of Harrison on the hall table was playing havoc with her equilibrium?

She stared at it, trying to view it objectively. It was just a face, after all. The features weren't particularly even—the eyes were too cold and the jaw much too harshly defined ever to be called handsome. The photographer had caught him smiling, but it wasn't a sunny, happy smile. It was nothing but a cynical upward curve of those hard, sensual lips.

Kimberley turned away from the photo, removed her coat, and set to work immediately. She'd tied her hair back and was wearing a pair of ripped jeans with her oldest T-shirt, which seemed to have shrunk slightly with repeated washing. Once black, it was now a sort of washed-out grey colour, and it revealed about two inches of her midriff.

She couldn't find a mop, so she filled up a bucket with hot soapy water and set about cleaning the floor the old-fashioned way—on her hands and knees!

There was something curiously relaxing about seeing the floor clean up beneath her cloth. Her busy life in London meant that she employed someone else to clean her house, but actually it was really quite satisfying to do it yourself, she decided—if you had the time.

She was just about to wring out her cloth when she heard the kitchen door open. Kimberley looked up, expecting to see Mrs Nash, her smile of greeting fading into frozen disbelief as the longest pair of legs she had ever seen swam into her field of vision. She let her gaze wander up into a hard and cruel face.

And the cold grey eyes of Harrison Nash.

CHAPTER TWO

'WELL, well, well—how the mighty have fallen,' came the sardonic drawl.

His voice sounded exactly the same—rich and deep. And as contemptuous as it had ever been. Kimberley dropped the cloth and it splashed water on to the front of her T-shirt.

'Do you know,' he continued, in that same, silky tone which sent prickles of excitement and dread down her spine, 'I rather like to see you in such a *subservient* position, Kimberley? Rather fetching. And, funnily enough, I was never particularly turned on by wet T-shirt competitions—but I can now see that I'm going to have to revise my opinion.'

His cool grey gaze had travelled to her sopping T-shirt, where the water had cruelly outlined the rounded swell of her breasts with detailed precision. Under his gaze she felt the nipples tighten immediately into those exquisitely painful little peaks, and she felt a hot weakness kick at the pit of her stomach. She saw the flash of hunger which darkened his eyes and he moved the tip of his tongue over his lips in a gesture which shrieked pure provocation.

Remember what he did to you.

'What the hell are you doing here?' she demanded as she flung the cloth back into the bucket and scrambled to her feet.

'I really should be asking you that question, don't you think? Are times hard for merchant bankers? Supplementing your income with a spot of charring——'

'My mother happens to do the charring in this house,' she cut in icily. 'God knows why she does it, but she does—and I will *not* have you insulting her.'

'I wouldn't dream of insulting your mother, whom I both like and respect.' His eyes narrowed; she could barely see them. 'Unlike her little madam of a daughter. Tell me, did you hatch a plot to get back into this house, somehow—anyhow? What are your intentions—to try to ruin Duncan's life a second time?'

Kimberley stared at him, wondering genuinely if his memory was defective. 'You're mad! What are you talking about?'

'I'm talking about your motives for being here.'

'My *motives*? You really aren't making yourself at all clear, I'm afraid, Harrison.'

'Then allow me to elucidate,' he said softly. 'My brother is returning from America, where he went after you dumped him, and he's bringing with him his new fiancée. And now you're here. Again. I'm just interested to know what you're up to. Do you want him back? Or do you just want to rub in what's he's been missing all these years? Are you planning to flaunt that beautiful, hot, rapacious little body around him?'

'You *are* mad,' she said scornfully. 'If your memory serves you as well as mine, you will recall that *you* were the one determined to break our relationship up.'

He gave her a ruthless little smile. 'You think so? If you'd really loved him you'd have told me to go to hell! As a matter of fact, that's what I expected to happen.'

Kimberley's eyes narrowed suspiciously. '*Expected*? Are you telling me that you were calling my bluff? That it was some kind of little test which I had to pass to be allowed to marry your brother?'

He inclined his head. 'If you like. When a rather wild young man—who stands to inherit the kind of money Duncan will one day have—announces he's about to marry, it's wise to put the commitment of *both* partners to the test.'

It was unbelievable! The man was living in the Dark Ages! Kimberley shook her head slowly and incredulously. 'Did your mother know this—that you were conducting this barbaric little experiment?'

He gave her a bored smile as he ignored her question. 'As I said—I expected to be sent away with a flea in my ear. Instead of which you went out of here clutching a big, fat cheque in your greedy little hand. But that was nothing to what you very nearly gave *me*. Was it, Kimberley?' he mocked.

Kimberley blushed scarlet. Only someone as hateful as Harrison Nash would take such pleasure in reminding her of her behaviour that day.

He moved a little towards her and instinctively she stiffened, her head held proudly high, her eyes slitted into glittering blue shards.

'So what did you spend the money on, hmm? Easiest bit of money *you* ever made in your life, wasn't it, Kimberley?' He gave an empty-sounding laugh. 'My God—you stand there so cold and so damned beautiful, as though ice were running through your veins instead of blood, and yet I only have to touch you and you go up in flames—don't you? Tell me, Kimberley, do all men have that effect on you, or is it just me? It could prove quite embarrassing, surely?'

She fixed him with a frosty smile, though her heart was beating like a bass-drum in her ears. 'I rather think you overestimate your own attraction, Harrison.'

He gave a half-smile. 'You think so? Perhaps I do, but I'm pretty confident in your case. Maybe we should put it to the test.'

She saw the hungry intent on his face, and understood his meaning immediately. 'Don't you dare try!'

He came one step closer, totally ignoring what she was saying. 'But you want me to, don't you, Kimberley? We both know that. You hate me, yet you want me...' He pulled her into his arms, not roughly but not gently either.

'If you dare continue, then I'll scream as loudly as——'

There was no scream. Not even the smallest attempt at resistance, which would have left her with some dignity. But there was no resistance, and no dignity. Just an overpowering reaction to him which took all her will away, sapped her strength and her resolve and left in their place the swamping, unbearable cocktail of desire and frustration as she let him kiss her.

And, as she'd done once before, she opened her mouth wide beneath his—so wide because she wanted to eat him up, to lick him all over. She gave a little moan as she found her hands winding themselves around his broad back, and she clung on to him as though she were clinging to life itself.

'Oh, baby,' he murmured into her mouth. 'Yes. Show me. Show me just how much you want me...'

She didn't know what he wanted her to do. She was responding through pure instinct, kissing him back with frantic fervour as though she had never before been kissed. As indeed she hadn't.

Not like this.

'Or shall I show you?' he whispered, and pulled her into him, as close as it was possible to be. She felt his arousal immediately; no garment in the world had yet been designed which could disguise how hard and hot and turned on he was.

Her hips swivelled in instinctive excitement against him, and he gave a low laugh. 'You want that, don't you? Don't you?' He kissed her again, and one hand slid to her back, underneath her T-shirt, and he rubbed his hand sensually against the silky bareness of her skin, a soft, tantalising caress, a tiny circular movement which cajoled an instinctive response, and she felt as though her veins were being transfused with thick, sweet honey.

'Oh, baby.' He dropped his head to whisper against her hair. She felt him shudder—such a wild and uncontrolled shudder of excitement—and it made her realise that he teetered on the very edge of control. She pulled away from him, afraid of what might happen if she didn't. He stopped kissing her immediately, and she almost gasped as he stared down at her, for she barely recognised him, the stark hunger on his face turning him into a stranger.

But he *is* a stranger, she thought. What do you know of Harrison Nash, other than the fact that he represents nothing but a wild and elemental danger?

'You were wise to stop me,' he said, in a flat, deliberate voice. 'Because I'm afraid that if we carried on kissing then I would not have been responsible for my actions. Much more of that and I would have been unable to stop myself from removing every single item of clothing from that beautiful body of yours and taking you right here, because all my reason seems to have deserted me.'

And then he shook his head in some kind of despairing disbelief. 'Dear God!' he exclaimed. 'What am I *saying*? What am I *doing*? My mother could have walked into the kitchen. The gardener's outside——'

She'd had enough of his self-disgusted confession, and every word he uttered only added to her own despair. 'Let me go——'

'No.'

She stared up at him, her mouth quivering, on the brink of tears. 'Harrison, *please*.'

His eyes narrowed at her trembling state. 'Kimberley—this thing between us——'

She shook her head distractedly, as if trying to remove a very heavy burden which simply refused to budge. 'It's sex!' she asserted. 'Nothing but sex! That's all. Just some unfortunate accident of nature—a chemistry between two people who happen to loathe one another. And I *hate* it, if you must know.'

His eyes were bleak with self-loathing. 'You can't hate it any more than I do,' he said bitterly.

She tried to pull away, but he still held her firm, and her determination to escape him was only rivalled, infuriatingly, by the desire to give in—to him, and to herself. To give herself up to the white-hot passion which threatened to devour her. 'Will you please let me go now?' she asked quietly.

'Only if you promise not to run away.'

'I'm promising you nothing. You have no right to ask anything of me.'

'Not even to leave Duncan alone?'

She could have wept. That he could have started to make love to her, yet still think her duplicitous enough to imagine that she would scheme to steal Duncan from his new fiancée. 'Oh, for goodness' *sake*! It's all over! It's history!'

'You mean you no longer care about him?' he asked quietly.

'That's right,' she answered, equally quietly.

'But maybe you never did care?' he challenged, in a voice of pure steel.

She took a deep breath. She wanted him to despise her so much that he would be repulsed by her. To hate her so much that he would never try to touch her again. And if he never touched her again she would be safe from the power he wielded over her. 'Sure, I cared for Duncan,' she said, in the husky kind of voice she'd heard bimbos use. 'But maybe I cared about the money more. You did me a big favour, Harrison. Does that make you feel better?'

His mouth became an ugly line. 'God, you are nothing but a little bitch,' he ground out. 'And if I ever doubted whether I'd done the right thing in trying to buy you off, you've just convinced me.'

Her cheeks flamed. Knowing that his rejection of her was the only sure route to sanity was one thing, seeing that look in his eyes was another.

'So, was it worth it, Kimberley?' he asked, still in that cold, scornful voice. 'Did the money I gave you compensate for any fleeting regrets you might have had that you'd made the wrong decision?'

She picked up her handbag from the table. 'I think that we've exhausted the whole subject. I'm going now, Harrison. I can't say that it was nice seeing you again, because I'd be lying. I'll leave it to you to explain to your mother why I can't continue with the cleaning. I'm sure you'll think of something.'

His voice was soft; it echoed in her ears as she left the room. 'There's only one thing that I can think of right now, and that's how much I want you, Kimberley. As much as you want me.

Whichever way you look at it—there's unfinished business between us.'

She composed her face, then turned. 'In your dreams, Harrison,' she said coldly. 'Goodbye.'

CHAPTER THREE

KIMBERLEY left Brockbank House mixed up, het up and downright angry with herself at the way she'd handled Harrison. To say nothing of the way he'd handled her—both literally *and* figuratively, she thought disgustedly.

She walked home by a circuitous route, and by the time she'd reached her mother's cottage she had calmed down enough to realise that she hadn't hurt more than her pride—and since only one person knew about it, and she wasn't planning on seeing him again, then, so what?

She had managed to avoid him successfully for two years, and if she managed to avoid him for the rest of her life, then the situation need never arise again. He rarely visited Woolton—she knew that. He was only here now, she presumed, because Duncan was bringing over his new fiancée to meet the family, and once he'd celebrated the engagement Harrison would be off again, to France or Germany or wherever it was he lived, pulling off the kinds of huge deals her mother kept harping on about.

The way to avoid him would be simple. She might actually have to come clean with her mother. Not exactly telling her the *whole* truth—that would be far too upsetting—but perhaps explaining to her that for very personal reasons she simply couldn't

stand the man, and she would like to be informed
if he was planning any trips home. Then she would
just avoid setting foot in the village to visit her
mother until he was safely on his way again.

And, for the moment, she wished for two things.
That her mother's ankle would heal very quickly,
so that she could escape from the danger of his close
proximity. And that something horrible would
happen to Harrison Nash. Perhaps he could go bald
and lose all his money?

Kimberley bluntly told her mother that she had no
intention of cleaning the Nashs' house while
Harrison was there. 'Let him do it!' she declared.

Mrs Ryan had been brought up in a very different generation from her daughter. 'But he's a
very important executive, dear,' she said
reprovingly.

Kimberley glowered. 'And so am I, Mum. So am
I!'

The next couple of days passed uneventfully. She
took her mother out for long drives, she cooked
meals, and they had companionable chats over a
couple of glasses of wine in the evenings.

She saw Harrison just once—when she went
shopping one day and spotted him just pulling to
a halt in the fiendishly expensive black car which
had nudged her out the fast lane on the motorway
the day she'd arrived. She should have guessed it
was *him* at the wheel of such an outlandishly
expensive piece of driving equipment, she
thought resentfully.

She saw him climb out. He wore black jeans and a black polo-neck sweater, with a black leather jacket protecting him against the cold of the December day, and he looked suitably diabolical, thought Kimberley. He was unshaven, and the thick black hair was ruffled by the breeze. He glanced up and her heart seemed to still with the sheer physical impact of his presence. It was like being given a solid punch to the solar plexus, robbing her of air and of comfort, and then, suddenly and devastatingly, he smiled.

There was no malice in that smile today, not even desire. Kimberley would have challenged anyone in their right mind to have resisted that smile, and she had to fight hard with herself to maintain the cool, haughty look she was giving him. Yet she couldn't look away; something kept her staring at him.

She felt the wind lift up the heavy silken tresses of her hair, and it tugged at the hem of the short tartan mini-skirt she wore, revealing the slim length of her thighs, encased in ribbed woollen tights. She saw the dark eyebrows rise fractionally, and she turned hastily and almost ran into the local grocery store.

Conversation stilled immediately. It was a small enough village for memories to be long, and Kimberley's inexplicable jilting of Duncan had kept the locals in gossip for a good few months.

After replying politely but in a restrained manner to the curious questions of Mrs Spencer—the owner—she had bought her eggs and her bread, and the fresh fruit her mother had asked for, when the tinkling of the shop-bell behind her announced that

someone else had come in behind her. She only had
to look at the barely concealed excitement on Mrs
Spencer's face to know just who that someone was.

'Can I help you, Mr Nash?' asked Mrs Spencer
obsequiously.

'No, thanks,' came the deep voice. 'I came to
give Miss Ryan a hand with her shopping.' The grey
eyes were shuttered. 'I'll give you a lift home,
Kimberley.'

He thought that he had her out-foxed. He was
probably assuming that she cared too much for
what others thought of her to resist him, that she
would meekly agree to the lift.

Well, he was wrong.

'I have my own car, thank you,' she answered
coolly. 'I've never had to rely on men for lifts.'

His mouth quirked a little. 'Very commendable.
I'm sure that you make a lot of men feel very re-
dundant. And I realise that you have your own car,
but you've left it sitting outside your mother's
house. It's a small red thing, isn't it?'

Calling Kimberley's beloved MG a 'small red
thing' was tantamount to asking her if she knew
how to change a plug, and her breathing quickened
in temper.

'It's a damn sight better than that ridiculous
monstrosity which you drive!' she retorted. 'But
then women don't have the need to use a car as a
substitute for any areas in which they might be—
er—*lacking*.'

She had allowed herself to get carried away, and
as soon as the words were out she regretted them—
not just because Mrs Spencer was bristling with un-

disguised indignation, though frankly Kimberley doubted whether she'd actually got the gist of what she'd been saying, but also because Harrison's sickeningly sardonic smirk left her in no doubt that he knew and *she* knew that he didn't have any areas in which he was lacking.

'Are you quite sure you won't change your mind?' he mocked softly, and Kimberley knew that he wasn't just talking about giving her a lift home.

She blushed madly. 'No, thank you,' she reiterated. 'I'll walk.'

She heard Mrs Spencer's sharp intake of breath, as though she was indignant that someone like her, a little Miss Nobody, should have the temerity to turn Mr Nash down—and on more than one occasion!

'You can't walk—it's started to rain.'

He didn't give up, she would say that for him. She knew exactly what he wanted—to get her in his car so that he could begin to seduce her again. At least here, in the shop, she was safe from that. And she doubted that Harrison would be desperate enough to follow her home. Ice-blue eyes were turned disdainfully and decisively in the direction of the grey glitter of his. 'I don't care. I like the rain.'

His eyes flickered over the brief little tartan mini, with its short matching jacket. 'I'm quite sure you do. But, exquisite though you may look, you're hardly dressed to combat the elements,' he said softly.

'Let me be the judge of that!' she answered coolly, and walked out of the shop.

He walked directly behind her, staying her with a hand on her arm, and she had to steel herself not to respond to the fleeting contact. He bent his head close to her face, and she was caught up in the dazzle from those glittering grey eyes. 'I told you,' he said softly, 'that we had some unfinished business to settle.'

'Oh, go to hell!' she said exasperatedly, infuriated when he laughed at her, and she stalked off in the direction of her mother's.

Even so, she wondered if he'd follow her. But he didn't, and she walked home with the steady drizzle slowly soaking the woollen fabric of her suit until it clung to her in a soggy mass. Her hair was dripping; the egg-box was drenched, and the bread was virtually inedible—but her mother hardly noticed; she was bobbing up and down with excitement when Kimberley walked through the door.

'Should you be hopping around on your bad ankle like that?' observed Kimberley mildly.

'Oh—it's almost better, darling. Dr Getty says I'm as fit as a flea. Listen—they've just delivered an invitation from Brockbank. Margaret Nash is throwing a party to celebrate Duncan's engagement tomorrow night. I'm invited—and so are you!'

Kimberley put the shopping on the kitchen table and eyed the invitation her mother was proffering. 'I'm not going,' she said flatly.

Her mother's face fell. 'Oh, Kim—why ever not?'

Kimberley sighed. 'Just think about it, Mum. If I go it'll just put people's backs up—especially his new fiancée. I'm sure that if I were her I wouldn't particularly want his ex-fiancée turning up. People would be bound to make hurtful comparisons—and I don't expect that Duncan would want to see me either. In fact, I'm surprised that I was included on the invitation.'

But she wouldn't even admit to herself the real reason why nothing would make her set foot inside Brockbank House again.

'You go. You'll have a great time.' Kimberley picked up a towel and began to rub at her sopping hair. 'Will you ring up and RSVP for me?' she asked. 'Please?'

Mrs Ryan's eyes narrowed. 'I've a feeling there's more to this than meets the eye, but, yes, darling—if you're absolutely adamant.'

'I am.' She stared down at her mother's ankle. 'And if you're feeling better now, Mum, then I'll have to think about getting back to London.'

Mrs Ryan sighed. 'I can't say I wasn't expecting it. Such a pity, though—I could quite get used to having you around the place again.'

Kimberley had planned to leave the following afternoon. She had just finished packing after lunch when there was a knock at the front door. Thinking it might be her mother, who had insisted on hobbling next door to see her neighbour, just to prove she could do it, Kimberley opened the door. Before her stood a young woman in her early twenties—someone Kimberley didn't recognise.

She had shiny shoulder-length fair hair, which was cut into a bob, and she wore a superbly cut pair of trousers in an immaculate but very unseasonal cream colour, with a matching cashmere jacket. Gold gleamed discreetly at her ears and neck and she exuded a kind of confidence which only money could give you. And lots of it, too.

'Can I help you?' asked Kimberley uncertainly.

The girl creased her eyes into a frown. 'Are *you* Kimberley Ryan?' Her voice was American—cultured and direct.

'Yes, I am—but I'm afraid I don't——'

'I'm Caroline Hudson—I'm Duncan's fiancée. Would you mind awfully if I came in?'

Kimberley pulled herself together and opened the door wider. 'Of course I don't mind. Do come in.'

The American girl immediately stepped over the threshold.

'Won't you sit down?' asked Kimberley politely, not at all sure about the etiquette of entertaining your ex-fiancé's fiancée. 'And have some tea?'

'Thank you. I will sit down, but I won't stay for tea.' Caroline positioned herself in one of the comfy armchairs and began fiddling with the gold link bracelet at her wrist.

Obviously, thought Kimberley, she wasn't quite as confident as she had initially seemed. She wondered why the girl had come. She strove to say something neutral which couldn't possibly be taken the wrong way.

'That's an absolutely beautiful ring you're wearing,' she managed.

It was obviously the right thing to say, because Caroline smiled as she held her left hand up to the light in the manner of newly engaged women the world over and the mammoth diamond solitaire sparkled and glimmered magnificently. 'Isn't it?'

she agreed. 'We bought it in Tiffany's. Duncan wanted me to have the family ring—but I wanted something new. I didn't,' she said deliberately, 'want the ring that you'd worn.'

Kimberley nodded. 'That seems like a very wise idea.' She looked questioningly at the American girl. 'Do you want to tell me why you've come here?' she asked gently.

Caroline nodded, then fell silent before turning her rather spectacular green eyes anxiously to Kimberley. 'You aren't in love with Duncan any more, are you?'

Kimberley was so surprised that she almost laughed aloud, but then, realising that that could be taken as offensive, shook her head emphatically instead. 'Heavens, no! Hand on heart. That was over a long time ago, and to be quite honest I think that was the best thing for both of us.'

'So do I,' said Caroline firmly. 'Duncan's told me about you. I know you're brighter than he is, and I know you're ambitious—it would have meant that he would always have been competing against you, and he couldn't have coped with that—not in the long run. He needs someone like me. I don't care about making my mark on the world and I've more than enough money through my trust fund— and if that sounds awful, then I'm sorry, but I can't help being rich. I'm quite happy to be Duncan's woman, to support him. That's what I want to do with my life.'

'Lucky Duncan,' said Kimberley faintly. 'But I don't quite see——'

'Duncan loves me—I know that. But——'
Caroline lifted her hands up in the air and the
bracelets at her wrist jangled like wind-chimes.
'How can I put it? I guess it's just that you're a
ghost he's never put to rest. And everyone else here
knows that you dumped him.' She saw Kimberley's
expression. 'I'm sorry—I didn't mean to insult you.'

Kimberley shook her head. 'Of course you didn't.
Please carry on.'

'It's just that if you don't come to our party tonight, it's going to become like a sort of *thing*—
you know how people are. They'll say that you
couldn't bear to see him, or that he couldn't bear
to see you. Maybe they'll think,' she finished miserably, 'that he's still in love with you.'

Kimberley looked at the girl who sat, her
shoulders hunched up now, in her mother's sitting-
room. Young, beautiful, rich—and bogged down
by all the insecurities of love. Damn love! she
thought vehemently. 'What is it that you want me
to do?'

'Come tonight,' urged Caroline. 'To the party.
And show there's no hard feelings—nothing bottled
up.' She looked up at the ceiling, then down again,
swallowing convulsively as she did so. 'I need to
see Duncan. With you. Do you understand what I
mean?'

Kimberley nodded. It seemed that Caroline
needed to put her own ghosts to rest. 'Of course I
do.'

'Then you'll come?'

Kimberley thought of Harrison, and of music,
imagined him in a dinner jacket, looking superbly

at home in the ravishing surroundings of Brockbank House. She put the thought firmly away. 'I won't stay very long,' she promised. 'But, yes, I'll come.' I owe Duncan, after all, she decided.

The heavy velvet drapes had been left undrawn and the lights of Brockbank blazed out, shimmering and sparkling from their costly chandeliers, to spill glorious light on to the gravelled drive leading up to the big house.

Kimberley drove, even though the distance was short enough to walk, but she wasn't planning to drink anything, not tonight, and with her car there she'd be able to make a hasty getaway. She had packed her suitcases and loaded them in her boot, and planned to drive straight to London from the party. 'And if I leave before you do,' she told her mother, 'then you can always get a taxi if you don't get a lift from anyone else.'

Kimberley had deliberated for ages over what to wear. There were so many things she didn't want to look like—a *femme fatale*, for one thing, or a defiant ex-lover who was pulling out all the stops to show how good she could look. On the other hand if she dressed like a total frump, for what was obviously going to be quite a smart do, it would be oddly out of character—and quite bad manners.

In the end she wore her black dress, which had seen her through just about every social occasion imaginable, and had never yet let her down. It came to several inches above the knee, but apart from showing some leg it covered everything else, with its high neck and long sleeves. The beauty of it was in the cut and the material. It was made of butter-soft silk, which rustled like a whisper as she walked.

Her hair she wore piled high upon her head, with several black corkscrew tendrils teased out to frame her face. With black kid slippers and pearls at her ears and wrists, she felt that she could withstand an hour or so at the party. And surely, in a crowd, it would be easy to avoid being alone with Harrison?

At first she saw neither brother. She was greeted at the door by Margaret Nash—who thanked her profusely for her help with the house—and by Caroline.

Caroline looked stunning—and nervous. She wore a slithery sheath of a dress in gleaming scarlet satin. She immediately took Kimberley to one side and took her wrap. 'Duncan's gone to order more champagne,' she whispered. 'I want to be here when he sees you.'

An awful, until now formless fear manifested itself. 'He does know that I'm coming?' asked Kimberley.

Caroline looked her straight in the face, her mouth a thin, determined line. 'No. He doesn't.'

Dear God, thought Kimberley despairingly, wondering how on earth she could get out of here.

'I couldn't see the point of telling him,' continued Caroline, apparently unconcerned by Kimberley's shocked silence. 'And neither could his mother.'

'His *mother*?'

Caroline nodded.

'I think you'd better explain,' said Kimberley faintly, feeling more and more divorced from reality by the second.

'His mother suggested it. Like me, she thinks it's a ghost he ought to lay to rest. You see, young love is very, very intense—and you were both so young when you were engaged. Added to that, rejection is so much harder to take when you're that young—by the time you're in your mid-twenties you've usually experienced a bit more of it, so it doesn't knock you quite so hard! And the person who rejected you assumes a much greater importance over the years than if the affair had just dwindled out naturally. Duncan needs to see you again, Kimberley. To see that you're not superwoman, that you're normal—just someone he used to know.'

It had the air of being a rehearsed speech. Kimberley was quite astonished, and couldn't help admiring the American girl's guts, but she felt bound to ask, 'You're taking a bit of a risk, aren't you, Caroline? What if it backfires on you?'

Caroline smiled. 'I'm a gambler—and I don't take unnecessary risks. Oh, my—here he comes.'

Kimberley automatically straightened her back, as though she were a soldier on parade, watching while Duncan wended his way towards his fiancée, a butler carrying a tray of champagne glasses following closely behind.

He hadn't seen her; she was concealed by the stoles and wraps which hung from the oversized coat-stand, and she had ample opportunity to observe him.

It was amazing how much two years had changed him, and in that time he had gone from boy to man. It shocked Kimberley to see how much he had changed, if only because it emphasised how very young he must have been when he asked her to marry him. He was dressed conservatively, in a well-cut suit, and his hair was short and neatly combed. He had the preppy look of someone who had been influenced by their environment—as obviously he must have been influenced by the country he had chosen to live in. His eyes rested fondly on Caroline, and the look shining from them told Kimberley everything she needed to know.

She stepped forward, a genuine smile on her face. 'Hello, Duncan,' she said quietly.

There was a moment's silence. She noted every emotion which passed in quick succession over his face. Part recognition, surprise, bewilderment and then, heart-warming, but heart-rending too—because she didn't think she really deserved it—a wry smile, which became wider. He put his hands on her shoulders, kissed both cheeks, and stood staring down at her. 'Kimberley,' he said. 'You're looking good.'

'So are you.' There were so many things she wanted to say to him, things she knew must remain unsaid—because if she told him she was sorry it would resurrect it all, and wasn't the past best left buried?

But it was as though Duncan could discern her mixed feelings, because he looked down at her, a glint of amusement in his eyes—such warm, uncomplicated eyes when you compared them to those of his older brother.

'Kimberley,' he said quietly. 'Would you understand if I said thank you—for doing me the biggest favour of my life?'

Kimberley nodded, a lump in her throat, knowing exactly what he meant. 'I would. And thank *you*, Duncan—for being so big about it.'

There was a rustle behind them. 'Have you met Caroline?' He was eager, proprietorial, as his beautiful fiancée stepped forward and he bent to place a brief but possessive kiss on her mouth.

'I have.' Kimberley smiled. 'She invited me. I do hope you didn't mind?'

Caroline was smiling the reassured and victorious smile of the woman who has got her man. 'Of course he doesn't mind, Kimberley—he doesn't mind a thing I do! Let's all go into the other room. And, Duncan—you must dance with Kimberley. I'll bet you have *heaps* to talk about!'

In the event they didn't; they survived on niceties but Kimberley knew that that had not been the purpose of the dance. The public show of unity, Caroline's smiling approval of their dance all served to show the assembled guests that there were no deep yearnings from the former partners. No broken hearts which hadn't healed. Everything was all right.

But not for long.

Kimberley became aware that they were being watched, and she didn't need to be psychic to know by whom. Some sixth sense had alerted her to his presence as soon as he'd entered the ballroom.

It was evident from the little buzz of whispered excitement that the most eligible bachelor had just walked into the room. Kimberley saw women actually preening themselves—saw bosoms being thrust out and stomachs sucked in. Saw women tossing extravagant curls around their heads like tempestuous young fillies.

She looked up into Duncan's face, and had opened her mouth to say that she wanted to go and find her mother when a deep voice, which was about as welcome as a heat-wave in the desert, penetrated her consciousness.

'Why, Duncan,' came the sardonic admonishment, 'I'd be careful if I were you. If you leave that beautiful fiancée of yours on her own much longer then someone might just whisk her away.'

Duncan dropped his hands from Kimberley's waist immediately, and looked around. 'Sure. Thanks, Harrison. I'd better go find her. Nice to see you again, Kimberley,' he said absently, and set off in search of Caroline.

'Excuse me,' said Kimberley, and made to push past him, but he stopped her with an arm of steel.

'You're not going anywhere.'

'Let me go,' she said desperately, as just the touch of him started that familiar aching.

The deep velvet voice was tinged with anger—restrained but unmistakable anger. 'But surely you want to dance with *me*, Kimberley? Or is it just Duncan that you want to turn those big blue eyes up at? What the hell do you think you're playing at?'

'As a matter of fact Caroline came to my house today and asked me to come. She wanted to make sure that Duncan only had eyes for her, which, as anyone can see, he patently has.'

'Oh, really?' he mocked.

'Yes!' she answered impatiently. '*Really*! And now can you go away and bore someone else with your nasty suspicious mind? And damn well take your hands off me——'

But he ignored her protests, pulling her into his arms to lock her against the warm and beckoning sanctum of his broad chest. His arms went about her waist, as lightly as Duncan's had done, but oh, the difference took all her breath away. She was aware of the weight of each long finger as it rested at the narrow indentation between her ribs and the gentle curve of her hips. The butter-soft silk, which had seemed such a good idea at the time, now mocked her with its insubstantiality—for it felt as though he touched her skin instead of her dress.

Her breath came short and painfully from her lungs, catching the back of her throat to dry her already dehydrated lips as he drew her body closer, so that she could feel the solid length of each strong, muscular thigh as it moved enticingly against hers.

'Harrison...' It was meant to be a plea; it sounded like a prayer.

He gave a soft, low laugh. 'Yes, I know. So let's show them, little temptress. Which brother you want so much it's nearly killing you.'

If her brain hadn't been so befuddled by his proximity then warning bells would have sounded at those cold, clipped words, but the words had been accompanied by his completely enfolding her waist in his arms, and by his head falling to rest on hers.

The magic of dance could bewitch you into believing what you wanted to believe, and this dance was more bewitching than any other, thought Kimberley as she drifted in time with him to the music. For within the outwardly decent boundaries of what constituted a slow dance there were many variations, which ranged from the innocent to the sensual ... and this dance was profoundly, shockingly sensual. But not just sensual—Harrison danced with such skill that for a moment there even seemed to be tenderness mingled with the voluptuous pleasure of his touch.

Or perhaps, thought Kimberley, she was confusing tenderness with propriety—they were, after all, in the middle of a dance-floor, exciting the interested looks of most of the county set—so he could hardly touch her with the undisguised passion he normally demonstrated towards her.

She tried to tell herself to leave, yet she was reluctant to move her head from his shoulder, where the material of his jacket rubbed softly against her cheek. She forced herself to straighten up, but that was even worse—she would have to confront those narrow grey eyes which gleamed with some unspoken message.

'Are you going to let me go now?' she whispered.

'No.'

'I'll struggle.'

'Try.'

'Scream, then.'

'I'll kiss you.'

'Oh, Harrison—why are you doing this?'

'Why do you think?' he asked softly.

She closed her eyes to shut out that speculative grey gleam. She tried to imagine how she would behave if Harrison were some tiresome executive she was dealing with. Reason might work.

She opened her eyes again, wondering what it was she read in the spark of those enigmatic eyes— was it humour, or challenge? Whichever—it made no difference. She put on her calmest voice. 'You're a very attractive man, Harrison——'

'I'm glad you've noticed.'

He'd deliberately misinterpreted her. 'What I mean is that there must be countless women in this room who are dying to dance with you—do you really have to resort to these caveman-like tactics?'

'It seems that with you I do,' he said softly, and his eyes glittered. 'Besides, I don't want to dance with anyone else. Just you.'

She forced herself to remember that the words meant nothing. This was just a different approach to settling that 'unfinished business' he'd spoken about. And it seemed that reason was totally ineffective against such a determined and single-minded man as Harrison. Plain speaking might work.

'Well, I don't want to dance with you,' she said decisively, marvelling to herself that lying could be this easy. 'So can we please stop this nonsense right now?'

With her question she gave a little shake of her head, and as she did so a lock of hair tumbled free and fell on to her mouth—which was sticky with scarlet gloss—and stayed there.

Immediately he lifted a finger and pulled it away from her lips, staring at her for a long moment with hard and brilliant eyes, and suddenly his whole demeanour altered. The soft, languid grace which had characterised his dancing up until then disappeared, and instead she saw him tense, his body become rigid, and as it did so his face acquired a taut and flinty look to it.

'You're absolutely right,' he said harshly. 'This "nonsense", as you so sweetly put it, has been going on for too damned long.' And, so saying, he clasped her hand firmly in his and led her off the dancefloor, through the crowds of dancers, past the curious eyes of the onlookers and out into the hall.

Kimberley looked around her wildly, waiting for someone to challenge him, stop him—to quit behaving as if it were perfectly normal for a man to drag a girl behind him as if they were still living in the Stone Age.

But no one did anything other than smile indulgently as Harrison led her through a series of rooms, until at last they were in the library.

She supposed she could have stopped him herself; she didn't ask herself why she hadn't until afterwards, and by then it was too late. She could have stopped him at any time, especially once they entered the realms of total fantasy, when he pulled aside a crimson velvet curtain to expose a wooden panel which, when touched, slid silently aside to reveal a spiral staircase. He pulled her inside before the panel slid shut to enclose them.

It was ridiculous, crazy—like something out of the adventure stories she'd read as a child—but still she kept her hand meekly in his, saying nothing, not even when the staircase terminated in a room at what was obviously the very top of the house.

And she couldn't even pretend surprise when she saw that it was a bedroom.

CHAPTER FOUR

KIMBERLEY snatched her hand out of Harrison's, and this time he made no demur, just let her.

She stared up at him, dark and tall and forbidding in the stark black dinner jacket and the slim-cut tapered trousers. His dark hair was very slightly ruffled—had she done that? she thought suddenly. Hadn't her fingers crept up to run themselves luxuriously through his hair during that dance? His eyes had an almost luminous brilliance as they studied her, waiting for her next move—but grey was essentially a cold colour, she reminded herself, and Harrison's eyes were well suited to his nature.

She realised that she had been expecting him to take her into his arms, confident that once he had begun to touch her there would be no argument from her about what he had in mind—and it was pretty obvious just *what* he had in mind. After all, you didn't bring a woman into a room with a huge double bed and little else if you wanted to talk about the weather!

'You're smiling,' he observed. 'What's amused you?'

'You have,' she answered coolly.

'Oh?' A black eyebrow lifted elegantly upwards.

'I had expected a little more subtlety from you. Does it usually work—this approach?'

'And what approach is that?' he asked softly.

'Dragging a woman into the nearest bedroom.'

'It isn't the *nearest*,' he pointed out infuriatingly. 'But it's the one where I can guarantee we won't be disturbed.'

His words, deep and sensual, full of some sweet, sexual promise, sent a reluctant shiver down her spine. 'You're assuming a lot, aren't you?' She was amazed at how calm, how controlled she sounded, just as if she was the kind of woman who was frequently being propositioned like this.

'Am I? Don't you like the room?'

Dark woods and crimson hangings, a bed-covering of gold and deep bright hues; it looked medieval—and so did Harrison, she realised, for he had unknotted and removed his bow-tie and was now in the process of draping his jacket over the back of a chair. Positively medieval, she thought, her mouth drying as she stood watching him. But it wasn't the clothes that made him look that way, it was that whole masculine and arrogant stance— the total lack of pretence. He wanted her, and...and...

'Would you have preferred the women's magazine guide to seduction?' he queried. 'The romantic, candle-lit dinner followed by the stilted offer of a nightcap? The soft music and the grappling on the sofa?' He smiled. It was a cold smile. 'Such a bore, don't you think?'

'You cynic,' she said disbelievingly.

'But no hypocrite,' he parried softly.

The most unbelievable thing was that she was actually continuing the conversation, actually enjoying the mental sparring in a perverse sort of way, instead of turning round and fleeing from him. 'Do you do this sort of thing very often?'

Her cool query seemed to surprise him. 'Never.'

'So what makes me different?'

Only one tiny fragment of her mind acknowledged what she wanted him to say—that he loved her, that she was the only woman in the world for him. But of course he didn't say it. Because, in his own words, he was no hypocrite. Nor a liar.

'You know why,' he said softly. 'Because you're a fire in my blood which refuses to be dampened. You know that. It can't go on like this. *I* can't go on like this any more. We have to have this one night together.'

One night. That was all he offered. No, he was certainly no hypocrite. She shook her head and made to turn away, but then he did touch her, catching her lightly by the shoulders to turn her to face him, and she revelled in the feel of him, almost as much as she reluctantly thrilled to the burning brilliance of his eyes.

He stared down at her, the intensity which hardened his features making his face seem like granite come to life. 'Tell me you haven't thought of me these last two years, Kimberley, and I'll call you a liar,' he whispered softly. 'Tell me you haven't tossed in your bed at night, reliving that very first kiss and wanting me to kiss you again but this time not to stop. I want you, Kimberley—God, help me—I want you as I've never wanted a woman before.'

She recoiled even as she was enthralled by the stark statements. Hating him, yet wanting him, too. 'But I don't even like you . . .' she said brokenly.

His eyes hardened into slivers of grey metal. 'I know that. You've made that abundantly clear. But liking has nothing to do with us—or this. *This* . . .' And he shuddered as his mouth sought hers.

It was the end—or the beginning, whichever way she cared to look at it, and she couldn't even pretend that he'd forced his lips on hers because he hadn't. She had turned her face up to his eagerly and of her own volition, entranced by that raw and harsh entreaty.

He kissed her hard, passionately—not even bothering to disguise the depths of his ardour—and she kissed him back in kind, opening her mouth to him like a flower to the morning sun. She knew one brief moment when she tried to tell herself that it was not too late. That if she pulled away now and walked out of that door he would not stop her. But she knew she would not walk away, for he had spoken nothing but the truth to her. She *had* thought about him, tossed in bed, dreamt of him and wanted him, like this.

And what was he offering her? Very little. One night—nothing more. To damp the fire in his veins; to free him from the curse of wanting her. So might it not do the same for her? Leave her free to lead a normal life, instead of existing in the self-imposed isolation she'd sought because Harrison had haunted her mind and her senses for so long?

He broke away and, incredibly, he was smiling. A sweet, soft smile, more insidiously enticing than the hard, heated pressure of his body, and Kimberley found herself smiling back, forgetting everything but the pleasure of the night to come.

'You're so beautiful, Kimberley,' he whispered softly. 'So very beautiful, with your hair as black as the night itself and your face pale as a moonbeam.'

But she had to put a stop to this; he was telling her everything she wanted to hear, but she was in danger of reading more than he intended into his soft words of seduction. She wound her arms around his neck, pressed her body sinuously close to his, her mouth against his ear. 'Isn't that starting to sound like the women's magazine guide to seduction?' she whispered huskily, echoing his own words of earlier. 'And didn't you say you found that boring?'

For a moment she felt him stiffen and grow rigid beneath her touch, and then it was gone and he pushed her away from him, his face a series of hard, unreadable planes and shifting shadows, the eyes now less brilliant than opaque. 'Boring?' His hand slid round to the back of her dress and slid the zip down in one fluid movement. 'Sweetheart, the last thing you're going to be tonight is bored.'

The dress pooled around her ankles with a silken whisper, but Kimberley's heart beat a little faster— not at the exultant look of pleasure which hooded his eyes as she stood before him wearing nothing but her underclothes but at the almost cruel indefinable note in his voice as he made that last statement.

A small sound escaped his lips as his gaze devoured her, and, strangely, she wasn't shy. She liked it. Liked seeing that hungry, almost awestruck look on his face. He was, she realised, with a sudden flash of insight, as much at her mercy as she was at his. Uncaring of her semi-nakedness, she stood before him in her scarlet silk and lace until he took her into his arms.

She felt that he was quite fierce with excitement—kissing her on a long sigh, his hand moving up to unclip her hair so that it spilt in streams of black satin over her pale shoulders. With slow, sure fingers he massaged her back, gradually moving his hand round—but taking forever to reach her breast. And then it was her turn to make a helpless little throaty assertion, to shudder as his fingers traced tiny circles closer and closer to the nipple, until they both grew impatient with the costly bra, and he moved his hand round to her back, unclipped it with a single movement, so that her breasts fell out and against him, and the soft mounds were crushed against his chest.

He moved her away from him, studied both the pale, swollen globes so that they tightened almost unbearably under his lingering scrutiny, then bent his head and began to suckle at one tingling erect nipple. A sharp dart of pleasure pulled deeply at her womb.

'Harrison!' she whispered helplessly. Stop this, she wanted to say, though she was powerless to say it as she glanced down at his dark head at her breast. She hadn't known... No one had told her... That it was going to be this intimate, this beautiful...this special.

He kissed her while he removed his own clothes, one by one. Instead of feeling embarrassed, as his magnificent body was gradually revealed, Kimberley felt instead a mixture of heady pleasure and anticipation—for hadn't she lived this scenario in her dreams, a thousand times over?

He kissed her while he unbuttoned his shirt, and she helped him take it off, eager to feel the silk of his bare skin against her fingertips, and as she slid her hands down to rest against the hair-roughened chest she heard him make a small sound of delight as he deepened the kiss still further.

His ardour fuelled hers, so that she let him push her down on to the softness of the silken rug.

He kissed her from mouth to breast, over and over again. His lips found her eyelids, her cheeks, her shoulders, the tiny warm, soft crook of her elbow, and each of these he kissed, anointing her with the soft caress of his mouth.

She saw the brilliance in the grey eyes as he knelt over her, before his mouth began to explore her body, to seek out every centimetre as if he were paying homage. His tongue found the dip of her navel and her head fell back as he began to trace a wet path to her panties. And then she waited, her apprehension only surpassed by her breathless anticipation of what he was going to do next.

He hooked his fingers at the edge of the flimsy little garment and tore the delicate scarlet lace apart with a gentle ripping sound, and the thought of his scant disregard for the expensive piece of underwear sent her trembling anew with excitement.

She saw him smile as the discarded garment fell unnoticed to the floor and his gaze fell to the lush, creamy bloom of her naked body. She gasped with shocked excitement as he pushed her thighs gently apart with his fingers and dipped his head to kiss the soft fuzz of hair.

'No,' she begged him, but her body was trembling with delight.

'Oh, yes,' he whispered, before his tongue found that aching, delicate spot and he started to lick her with slow, pleasurable sweeps of his tongue, over and over again, until she realised that he was taking her down a path from which there could be no return.

'No!' she said again, on a broken note of protest, but it was already too late, and she moved with disbelief as she felt waves of pure pleasure tantalise her, rock her, until they finally engulfed her and she exploded against his mouth, sobbing as he caught her and pulled her into his arms.

She felt helpless, hopeless, vulnerable, shaking in his arms as her climax subsided, and he soothed her by stroking her all over again, until the delicious warmth began to build up once more, and Kimberley began to play with his nipples, to suckle them exactly as he had hers.

She looked up once and stole a glance at him. He had his eyes closed, a look of such exquisite rapture on his face that she grew bolder, her fingers moving down to touch him as intimately as he had touched her, and her breath caught in her throat with the pleasure of her first touch... Oh, it was enchanting to be able to touch him like this.

She felt him shudder beneath her fingers as she experimentally began to stroke him, waiting until he grew more and more aroused, then, wanting to taste him as he had tasted her, she bent her head, took the potent fullness of him in her mouth... She heard him give a groan of pleasure before she felt herself being gently but decisively moved away, and he scooped her up to lie on top of him.

'No,' he said firmly.

'Oh,' she protested.

He laughed. 'Did you happen to read up a textbook about every man's ideal fantasy woman? Because, if so, I think maybe you might have skipped a chapter, my sweet. I don't want any substitute—not this first time. I've dreamt about this far too long to want anything other than the real thing, Kimberley. You.'

'But you did it to me,' she pointed out. 'So why not?'

He looked very definitely surprised at her persistence. She could read a mixture of things in his eyes—arousal, amusement, and—yes, definitely— he was a little bit *shocked*!

'That wasn't supposed to happen,' he said wryly, circling her proud nipple with one long finger. 'You just happen to be *very* responsive...' And his mouth found hers.

But only to you, she thought as she felt his nakedness beneath her, remembering other men who had tried to arouse her, who she hadn't even been able to bear kissing her.

'Oh, God, Kimberley!' he sighed as he tightened his arms around her naked waist. 'You're so gorgeous. *Gorgeous.*'

She could feel the tension and excitement growing, could feel herself growing dizzy with the pure delight of the touch she'd craved for so long. She could scarcely believe that this was happening to her, that she was lying in a tangled and naked heap with Harrison. Her heart soared as he kissed her until the blood thundered in her ears, and she felt as though she would die unless he took her. Daringly she shifted her body slightly, so that she was lying directly over him, and now only one movement, one tiny little movement, was separating them from the ultimate intimacy.

'Let's go to bed,' he whispered urgently, but for answer she pushed her hips provocatively against his. Through her passion-glazed eyes she saw his own snap open, and a helpless look crossed the rugged features as he realised the fight was up.

'You witch,' he whispered softly against her mouth. 'You beautiful little witch.' Then he swiftly turned her over on to her back, all masculine arrogance and domination as he thrust into her with sweet, wild power.

Kimberley awoke in the bed, and as soon as she regained consciousness she remembered exactly where she was. Lying over her thigh was an unaccustomed weight... Harrison's leg—and the rhythmical sound she could hear beside her was Harrison's breathing.

She lay stock-still, holding her breath, afraid that he might be able to sense by instinct alone that she was now awake. Because—she had to face it—he had guessed just about everything there was to know about her body during that long night of lovemaking. To think that she'd been a complete and utter novice before they'd started—now she felt fully qualified to be able to rewrite the Kama Sutra—and throw in a few extra chapters besides!

Her heart quickened. She had never dreamt that it would be so...so wonderful, blissful, heavenly—every single superlative in the English language, in fact. She'd actually lost count of the times he'd made love to her. And each time it seemed to become more special, more intense, the kisses deeper, gentler. She had found herself wanting to murmur sweet nothings into his ear, to tell him that he was the most wonderful man in the world, that she adored him. She wanted to invent silly names for him. She wanted to make him boiled eggs for breakfast! She was in love!

Oh, Kimberley! What have you done? Her glorious, glowing happiness disintegrated like an icecube dropped into a glass of boiling water. Just because *she* had become unbearably affected by last night it didn't mean that Harrison had. He had said 'one night'. Just because he had been so sweet and gorgeous and sensational during that one night it didn't mean that he was about to start prowling around jewellers' or estate agents' windows, or flicking avidly through Tupperware catalogues!

She had to think calmly.

And then she nearly screeched aloud as she remembered her car.

Her car!

Her scarlet sports car was at present sitting in the drive outside Brockbank House, drawing bold attention to the fact that she hadn't gone home last night and advertising to even the least discerning just how she had spent the last few hours.

She suppressed a groan as she glanced over to the bedside table where the luminous dial of Harrison's watch was just visible. It was four a.m.

Far better if she crept out and took the car back home to London now. If anyone saw her she could say she'd had a bit to drink and had slept it off. She would have to hope they wouldn't ask where.

The alternative was falling back to sleep and meeting up with Mrs Nash, Duncan and Caroline over the kippers and kedgeree.

And Harrison.

She glanced again at his naked sleeping form. Dragging herself away from him was going to be sheer hell, but it had to be done. If he'd decided that one night was enough she would be saving face by disappearing now, rather than having to undergo the humiliating experience of him saying goodbye to her in the morning—and meaning it.

Some dark emotion, as brutal as a physical assault, made her skin break out into an icy sweat. Had he meant it literally when he had said 'one night'? And if he had could she possibly bear it? She bit her lip very hard. There was no alternative— she would *have* to bear it. She swallowed as she determined that if he wanted nothing more to do with her, even though she might be breaking up in a million pieces inside, externally at least she would maintain her pride and her dignity. She certainly wasn't going to beg him to see her again.

Very carefully Kimberley wriggled out from beneath Harrison's leg and rolled over to the side of the bed, holding her breath to hear whether he'd wakened.

He hadn't.

She slid off the bed and shivered as the cool night air hit her naked flesh, and she narrowed her eyes in search of her discarded clothing.

Silent as the night itself she put her bra on and pulled the black dress over her head, before slipping her bare feet into her shoes. She would carry her stockings and suspender belt and... In the darkness she blushed as her gaze fell on the ripped panties, and as she bent to pick them up, her fingers quickly closing around the tiny crumpled ball of scarlet lace, she couldn't help giving a grimace of regret. To have him make love to her was one thing, but had she really needed to respond quite so uninhibitedly? Surely it couldn't be *right* for a virgin to feel intensely turned on by having her underwear torn off her?

'Send me the bill,' came a flat, drawling voice, and Kimberley glanced over at the bed to find a pair of very cold, speculative grey eyes watching her every move. Something in the harsh set of his face immediately made her frantic thoughts alight on his statement with confusion.

'Bill?' she demanded. 'What are you talking about?'

He put his hands behind his head and continued to subject her to that coolly impartial scrutiny. 'Send me the bill,' he repeated indifferently. 'For your underwear. I have to tell you that I'm not usually in the habit of ripping the clothes from a woman's body, but I'm afraid that you really do bring out the worst in me, Kimberley.'

It was the most damning testimony to their night together. And Kimberley was stung and hurt and horrified that she had had the naïvety to imagine that he might have woken to contemplate some sort of future with her.

She gave him the kind of empty smile she would have conferred on the lowest form of life. 'The feeling is entirely mutual,' she said coldly. 'I hate you, Harrison.'

'Not half as much as I hate myself, my dear. But, as I told you, what we have between us has very little to do with liking,' he added bitterly.

Cheapened and ashamed, she moved away, sick to the depths of her heart.

'Oh, Kimberley?'

She stilled, some foolish little hope flickering into doomed life inside her. 'What?' She turned to look at him, and the arrogant indifference on his face told her everything she needed to know.

'I'm afraid that you didn't really give me the chance to discuss this last night,' he said matter-of-factly. 'And ... Let me see—how can I put this without being offensive? In view of your *eagerness* to consummate the act, I assume you've already taken care of contraception?'

She froze, wanting to sob, to scream.

To die.

She stared at him. What the hell? She had already told him the ultimate lie; she had told him that she hated him. One more wouldn't hurt.

'Naturally,' she answered coolly, and left.

Left the room and, finding her handbag on a table in the hall, left the house and ran out, cold and despairing as she let herself into her tiny scarlet sports car, and drove to London as if the devil himself were pursuing her.

CHAPTER FIVE

KIMBERLEY lay on the bed perfectly still, waiting for the sickness to pass.

Outside the cherry tree, with its glorious snowy blossoms, danced in the light breeze of the perfect late April afternoon.

Morning sickness, she thought woozily, she could have coped with—this late-afternoon sickness did not fit in at all well with her timetable! Fortunately James, her boss, had been surprisingly accommodating—letting her evolve her own flexi-hours so that she started work at six in the morning and knocked off at between three and four, when the sickness usually started.

The doctor had told her that the nausea and vomiting she'd been having would probably ease off by the time she entered the second trimester, but she was nearly five months pregnant and it showed no sign of abating.

She remembered back to when she'd first discovered she was pregnant.

She had arrived back in London, sick and despairing over the disastrous incident with Harrison and feeling as though she'd lost every last vestige of pride. She knew that she could never see him again. But Christmas had been looming, and she couldn't possibly have left her mother in the lurch.

So, the following week, having mentally girded herself for a possible encounter with Harrison, whom she had assumed would stay on with his mother for Christmas, Kimberley had returned to Woolton. But he had not been there.

Harrison had returned to France the day after the party, according to her mother.

And, in a way, the finality of his abrupt departure had helped; she had known that there were no more false hopes to be cherished.

It had been a week after Christmas when Kimberley had experienced her first fears, and within a day—although she'd had no experience of such matters—she had known that she was pregnant.

She had found out for sure at the weekend and had spent almost all of the two days lying in bed, looking up at the ceiling while her mind had tried to take in the enormity of this event, which was going to change the whole pattern of her life.

She had decided within the first day that she was not going to tell Harrison. There wouldn't have been any point. He wouldn't have wanted to be troubled with the repercussions of his famous 'one night'—especially when that one night had been nothing but the settling of an old score with a sexual chemistry which had been too strong for either of them to resist.

She had doubted whether he'd want anything to do with a child born to a mother he despised, and so the only point of telling him would have been to try to get some kind of maintenance from him—

and she certainly wasn't going to grovel around asking for his money.

If she needed money she had enough of her own. But she wasn't going to need any money, because she had also decided something else that first weekend—that she was going to have her baby adopted.

The doctor had been surprised. Adoption was a fairly radical step, he'd told her—traumatic for the mother, to have to go through nine months of pregnancy then have to give the baby up. He had advised her that in these times a woman had a choice. But the choice which he had offered her had been one which she had passionately rejected without giving it more than a second's thought. She could not have killed her child—Harrison's child.

The doctor had gently asked whether she'd thought of keeping the baby herself, had said that society accepted single mothers these days.

She had thought about it, of course she had. But wouldn't keeping the baby be worse in the long run? Was it fair to bring a child up with one parent out of choice? A parent, moreover, who would need to work long hours to be able to support a baby? Wouldn't the child become a typical 'latchkey' kid, with all the inherent disadvantages? Ferried from pillar to post, dumped on childminders she wouldn't really know—perhaps wouldn't even trust?

She would do the best for her baby; she would have a happy and healthy pregnancy and then she would give the child up for adoption. Give it away to some nice, loving, childless couple who would be able to offer him or her so much more than she could.

And, apart from the doctor, James was the only person she'd told. The others at work and the girl-friends she met up with at her health club would find out soon enough, when she started to show. There was no point in telling anyone else, especially not her mother—for wouldn't it only break her heart to discover that she had a grandchild on the way then to have to say goodbye to that grandchild forever?

James had been super—utterly supportive and pleased that she would be going back to work.

There were only two things which Kimberley had insisted upon. The first was that James never talked to her about the baby. Talking about the baby only seemed to make him or her more real, and she knew that the more real it became the harder it would be for her to have to give it up. The second was that she didn't want *any* baby paraphernalia—no tiny mitts or bootees—for exactly the same reason.

Kimberley dozed on and off for an hour, until the sickness had gone, then got up and had a shower to try and wake herself up. She had dressed in leggings and a sweatshirt and switched on the TV, deciding idly that now that the sickness had passed she really ought to start thinking about getting something to eat, when there was a sharp ring on the doorbell.

Because it was still light, and because she hadn't got round to it, she hadn't put the chain on, and she opened the door without a thought, the blood draining from her face as she found herself staring at Harrison.

He was dressed formally in an amazing oatmeal-coloured suit, which looked like an Armani, but his hair was untidy and his silk tie had been loosened.

His eyes were glittering as they surveyed her but she could read nothing in his face. Absolutely nothing.

'May I come in?' he asked coolly, but there was a strange quality to his voice, an odd edge—something she should have recognised, but failed to do so.

The pounding of her heart had diminished enough for her to draw a deep breath—the intake of oxygen she needed—and answer him in the same cool fashion. 'What for? I doubt whether we've got anything that's worth saying to each other.'

His mouth twisted with derision. 'Quite. Talking was never our strong point, was it, Kimberley?'

The sensual implication behind his silky insult made hot colour flare at her cheeks and she began to close the door, but, like a character in a detective film, he inserted one elegant foot in the doorway, preventing her from doing so.

'What do you think you're doing? Get your bloody foot *out* of my door! This minute!'

The foot stayed where it was. 'I told you that I wanted to come in——'

'And I told you——' Her mouth dropped open as he moved her away from the door, let himself in and closed it softly behind him.

Kimberley began to panic as he walked down the hall and straight into the sitting-room as though he were an invited guest. All kinds of thoughts and fears were rushing to assail her—like, He couldn't possibly *know*, could he?

Well, could he?

He was looking around the room, at the vivid peacock-blue silk curtains and the matching cushions, which had been slung all over the deep, comfy rose-pink sofa. In a tall blush-coloured vase was an enormous spray of gypsophila, studded with pinks, breathtaking and fragrant. 'Hmm.' He gave a little nod. 'Elegant, but cosy. Exquisite taste, Kimberley. But then I always knew you would have.'

She neither wanted nor needed his approbation—so wasn't it rather pathetic that his obvious approval of her home should please her so much?

'What are you doing here? I thought you lived in France?'

'I did. But I've moved.'

'To—to—England?' she asked shakily.

He gave a cold smile. 'The very same—to London, to be even more precise.'

Kimberley's eyes widened. 'But why?'

Those mesmeric grey eyes glittered. 'I find that I have pressing—business—in England. Why else?'

The effort of trying not to alert his suspicions to her condition was nearly killing her. 'I still don't know why you're here—what the hell do you want?'

He gave a nasty smile, put his face mockingly close to hers, and her heart accelerated out of control as she thought that he was about to kiss her. 'That depends what's on offer,' he said, slightly unsteadily, and Kimberley realised what it was about him which was different—he'd been drinking.

Oh, he wasn't drunk—somehow she could never imagine Harrison out of control, nor losing touch with that formidable intelligence—but he had obviously drunk just enough to be reckless. She could see that from the dangerous glitter in the grey eyes, and suddenly she felt frightened. He must *not* find out. He mustn't.

'You've been drinking!' she accused.

He sat down in one of the chairs, unasked. 'Yeah,' he agreed. 'It's true. Drinking to forget the coldest little bitch I ever had the misfortune to meet.'

'Have you just come here to insult me?' she enquired politely, some instinct telling her that if she failed to react then he would leave her. And she needed him to leave her, just as soon as was possible, because she had just found that it was quite possible to hate someone very much indeed and yet to want them to pull you into their arms and never let you go.

'I've come to see how you are.' He laughed, and the sound of it sent a chill down her spine; it was an angry, bitter, empty little sound that tore at her soul. He stared at her consideringly, his head to one side. 'And now I've seen. You look terrible,' he said. 'Awful.'

'Thanks very much.' They were on dangerous ground here. He spoke the truth—she *did* look terrible—but he mustn't know the reason why.

She had been physically sick every afternoon for more than four months, so that instead of gaining a little weight in the first stage of her pregnancy she had lost it instead. And the sudden weight-loss was reflected in the sickly pallor of her cheeks. Even her raven hair had lost its usual glossy sheen, and she knew that the black leggings and white sweatshirt only emphasised her colourless appearance. The doctor had told her that lots of women lost weight in pregnancy, that there was no reason why the baby should be harmed, and that she wasn't to worry.

But of course she worried.

'I've seen you look better yourself,' she answered him tartly.

'Have you? When was that? When you left me, naked and wanting you, creeping out like a thief in the middle of the night? Had your conscience got the better of you, Kimberley? Did it sicken you to remember what we had done?

Lies, glorious lies. Her salvation lay in lies. Behind them she could hide her hurt. She shrugged her slim shoulders. 'Let's just put it this way—it happened, and it's best forgotten, wouldn't you agree?'

He smiled a cynical smile. 'And if I don't?'

Ignoring that, she stared down at him, hating the way that her heart lurched at the sight of him in her house, his long legs sprawled out with careless elegance. 'Do you want some coffee?' she said pointedly. 'Before you go?'

'No, I don't want any coffee. You know what I want. *You!*' he said deliberately, and his eyes narrowed and darkened with all the physical manifestations of sexual promise.

Her body responded as if she was on automatic pilot, her face flushing as her veins began to be flooded with the fierce heat of wanting him.

Did he see her weakening? Was that why he took the opportunity to reach up and pull her down on to the sofa beside him? For a minute she reacted on that same automatic pilot, her body softening and burgeoning as it came into contact with the hard sinews and magnificent muscular strength of him.

'I can't stop wanting you, Kimberley, do you know that? No matter what I do, the wanting won't go away—is it the same for you? Is it?'

As he spoke his mouth was kissing softly at her neck, his hands moving to brush lazily over the firm swell of her breasts and she felt them grow heavy with desire. She found that her body was pliant— soft and welcoming—as he pushed her back against the scatter-cushions, kissing her with the fervour and the hunger of a man who had never kissed before.

She went under like a drowning woman, the elemental fire of his desire transmuting into a white-hot and incandescent passion as she let him kiss her. She felt flooded, exhilarated, all reason leaving her as his mouth continued its deliciously rapacious plundering. Her hands were on his shoulders, pushing distractedly at his jacket, her palms flattening out over his chest. His small sigh of pleasure against her mouth was like pouring paraffin on to a blaze already nearly out of control, and Kimberley let her hand fall on to his lap, revelling in the hard throb as her fingers lightly brushed his arousal.

He said something shockingly profound beneath his breath and he moved his hand beneath her sweatshirt to stroke his way slowly up her bare midriff towards her breasts, and Kimberley froze.

They'd only spent one night together, and yet she knew that Harrison was better acquainted with her body after one night than another man would have been after thirty years. Every curve, every crevice, every centimetre he had explored with his hands and his mouth and the tensile length of his arousal. Some time during that long, wonderful night Kimberley had suspected that if he had had the means to do so he would have lain her heart and her soul and her body bare, too—such had seemed his desire to possess her totally and completely.

True, at almost five months a slight swell of the belly would have been normal, especially in a woman as slim as Kimberley, but her loss of weight meant that in fact she barely showed at all. But the difference was noticeable to *her* eye, and would be, she suspected, to Harrison's, too. And, quite apart from anything else, she had gone up a bra size since she'd become pregnant—at times she even had to go to bed wearing a bra, her breasts were so aching and swollen. He would surely be able to detect *that*?

She sat upright, and pushed him away. She had to get him out of here. And quickly.

He gave her a quizzical look, a satirical dark eyebrow raised. 'So what happened to make you change your mind?' he enquired, as if it didn't matter one iota to him. But she could see from the sharp lines of tension on his face that it was as painful as hell for him to stop now. And for her, too. But it was imperative that reason take precedence over the desire of a man who cared nothing for her.

'Changed my mind? You arrogant bastard! I hadn't made it up in the first place!'

'No? That's not the message I was getting.'

'Whatever message I send out you only ignore it and then damn well interpret it the way that *you* want to!' she accused him, knowing that it was unfair—and untrue.

'Oh, come, come, Kimberley,' he chided. 'That intelligence of yours does not marry very well with crass hypocrisy.'

She averted her eyes from the darkly handsome and mobile features. 'I'd like you to go now. Please.' She tacked the nicety on to the end, thinking that it might appeal to some deeply buried chivalrous streak in his nature.

It didn't.

'I'm not leaving until I've said what I came here to say.'

'I can hardly wait.' She stood up, wanting to put distance between them, going to stand by the window. The daylight had almost gone now, the white of the cherry blossom looking unnaturally bright in the gathering gloom of the dusk.

His eyes were watchful. 'I have a proposition to put to you.'

'*Another* proposition?' she enquired icily, remembering when he'd used those words on another occasion. 'Not more money, surely?'

'No,' he said heavily. 'Not more money.'

'Go on—I'm listening.'

'I want to see you,' he said huskily.

Violins threatened to start playing, but she put them on hold. 'See me?' Then, stupidly, or perhaps not so stupidly, because she needed to know just what he was suggesting, she asked him, 'What for?'

He gave his cool imitation of a smile. 'Whatever you like. Theatre. Dinner. Picnics at weekends. You know—the things which men and women usually do together.'

'And bed, presumably? You're forgetting bed.'

His eyes darkened in a predatory and feral gleam. 'Oh, no, Kimberley,' he said softly. 'I'm certainly not forgetting bed.'

For the first time she became fiercely grateful that she *was* pregnant, because the baby was protecting her from her own foolishness, in a way. For could she honestly put her hand on her heart and say that if she hadn't been pregnant she wouldn't have been tempted to go along with his cold-blooded request? And have her pride trampled into the ground and end up with a heart even more broken?

'Sorry,' she said indifferently, 'I'm not interested.'

There was a momentary bleakness which hardened his autocratic features, and it affected her far more than it should have done; he obviously wasn't used to having his propositions turned down. She would never know whether he would have tried to kiss her again in order to change her mind—probably not, she decided—because the doorbell rang.

He stood there, unmoving and cold, as if he'd been hewn from purest marble, and Kimberley went to answer the door, wondering who it was, and how she was going to get rid of Harrison before she broke down in front of him and gave it all away.

It was James. Carrying roses. Red roses. He grinned. 'Just saw these and——' He stopped when he saw the warning look in Kimberley's eye, and in a brainwave she knew how she could get Harrison out of her life for good.

'Oh, darling!' she cried expansively, and she took the roses from James's arms and planted a kiss on the side of his surprised face as she linked her arm through his. 'They're absolutely beautiful! But you shouldn't have done—you spoil me!'

She heard a soft footfall behind her and then, blinking a little, she turned, as if she'd completely forgotten all about the dark, towering man with the set face who stood in the doorway of the sitting-room, watching them. 'Come and meet an old friend of mine. Harrison—this is James Britton, my boss. James—I'd like you to meet Harrison Nash.'

The atmosphere was as brittle as peanut-crunch. Harrison gave something masquerading as a smile and took James's hand, giving him a terse nod. 'A short acquaintanceship, I'm afraid. I was just leaving.' He gave Kimberley a strange, fleeting look. 'Goodbye.'

He said it as though he meant it, and although this had been what she'd wanted, Kimberley suddenly felt an overwhelming sense of blind panic. 'I'll see you out,' she said desperately.

She followed him out to the front door, alarmed by the forbidding set of his shoulders, tempted—unbearably tempted—to tell him the truth. But, when he turned around, the disdain and scorn which were clearly etched on his face stopped her.

'Your *boss*?' he queried sardonically. 'You're sure as hell doing a great job for industrial relations!' His mouth twisted in distaste. 'Tell me, does dear James know that you were touching me up minutes before his arrival? He must either be exceptionally trusting or exceptionally stupid. Or both.'

The accusation stung her, hurt her more than words could express. 'How dare you?' she said between gritted teeth. 'I won't have James insulted!'

'It's *you* I'm insulting. *Sweetheart*.'

'Get out!'

'Don't worry. I'm going.' And he dropped his mouth to hers, briefly and brutally, that one kiss openly displaying all the contempt he felt for her. 'Thanks for the memory,' he said bitterly, and walked out.

James came to find her and said nothing for a moment as he took in her trembling lips, the tears which were spilling from her blue eyes like water from a dam whose floodgates had finally been opened. He put an arm around her, warm and comforting, and turned her face into his shoulder, letting her cry and cry until there were no tears left.

'It's all right,' he told her. 'It's all right.'

She raised her tearstained face to his and shook her head distractedly. 'No, it isn't,' she whispered. 'It's never going to be all right.'

'He's the father, isn't he?'

There seemed no point in denying it, and she didn't think she had the strength to deny it—besides which she'd uttered enough lies that afternoon to last a lifetime. 'Yes.'

'I didn't realise you even *knew* Harrison Nash,' said James drily. 'Are there any other bosses of multi-national companies you're keeping under your hat?'

'I—oh, *James*!' Kimberley gripped her abdomen, her eyes filling with tears again.

'For God's sake—what? Is everything all right?'

But in spite of the tears she was now smiling— a smile which threatened to split her face in two as she stared at James.

'What is it?' he repeated.

'I felt it!'

James frowned. 'Felt what?'

'The baby,' she said, on a note of wonder. 'James, the baby just *moved*!'

CHAPTER SIX

THE doorbell rang and Kimberley waddled to answer it, feeling like a whale—beached or otherwise! Only four weeks to go—four weeks which seem to stretch ahead of her like an eternity. She felt enormous. She *was* enormous!

After her early weight-loss she'd gone from strength to strength, and now had a bulge which her doctor joked would have made him bet on twins if he hadn't seen her scan for himself!

She peered through the peephole which James had insisted she have installed, blinking her eyelids in a mixture of horror and disbelief when she saw Harrison standing there.

She sagged back against the wall, biting her lip as she wondered what on earth he was doing here—but that didn't actually matter. What was important was that he left her alone. And what was vital was that he didn't see her.

The doorbell rang again—a sharp, impatient sound. Kimberley decided to ignore it, until she heard his deep drawl.

'It's all right, Kimberley—I know you're in. Your car is parked outside and your neighbour informed me somewhat peculiarly that you usually have a "rest" in the afternoon. I don't know whether that was her euphemism for describing what you and James Britton get up to, and frankly I don't care.

But whether he's in there or not, I'm not going anywhere until I've seen you.'

'You're the last person in the world I want to see! Go and take your horrible grubby mind and your nasty insinuations somewhere else!'

'Are you going to let me in?'

'No!'

'Then I may have to break this very attractive little door down. Pity about that.'

'Just *try*!' shouted Kimberley, bordering on hysteria now. 'And I'll have the law down here so fast——'

'Your mother sent me.'

This completely took the wind out of Kimberley's sails. 'My *mother*? Why would my mother send you?'

'She's worried about you.'

'But there's nothing for her to worry about!' Kimberley shut her eyes in horror, ashamed of her own deception, and yet there had seemed no other alternative at the time. She had rung her mother regularly, and written. But she had not been down to stay since the pregnancy had become impossible to disguise, even with the baggy and layered clothes she wore. She had told her mother that she was having to go to Paris some weekends. She had blamed pressure of work. And she hated living the lie. 'Why's she so worried?' Kimberley asked brightly. 'I'm fine.'

'Could the fact that she hasn't seen you for nearly four months have something to do with it?' he grated. 'Now, are you going to let me in or not?'

'No! I'll ring her tonight.'

His voice was impatient. 'I promised her I'd deliver a package to you in person.'

'Package?'

'It's your birthday present. From her. And there's a letter with it.'

'Can't you just leave it on the doorstep?' asked Kimberley desperately. 'I honestly don't want to see you, Harrison. Surely you can understand that?'

There was a short silence. 'Yes,' he said, in an odd and harsh-sounding voice. 'I can understand that. OK—I'll do as you ask and leave the package on the doorstep. But I gave her my word I'd speak to you, so promise me you'll go and see her?'

'I promise.' Now go, she thought. Please *go*.

Leaning back against the wall, her hands drawn protectively over the baby, she waited. And when she looked out through the peephole there was no sign of him.

Slowly and cautiously she opened the door, breathing quickly as she gingerly bent down to retrieve the brown paper package, since such movements were extremely uncomfortable in this late stage of pregnancy. She picked the package up and straightened herself, rubbing the small of her back with a weary hand, and found herself staring into a pair of disbelieving grey eyes as Harrison emerged from behind one of the cherry trees, now bloomless and covered with leaves.

She tried to make a dash for it, but she was too large and too cumbersome and he caught her wrist—not hard—but so firmly that she couldn't break free.

'Dear God,' he whispered in a strained voice. 'So this is why. This—is—why,' he repeated slowly, then seemed to come to his senses, like a man coming round after an accident. 'Dear God,' he said again.

Kimberley swayed and might have fallen had he not caught her by the waist. She saw her neighbour staring over at them curiously, thought what a peculiar sight they must make.

'Are you all right?' Harrison grated.

'I want to go inside,' she said shakily as, blindly, she pushed the door open, hardly realising where she was going, hearing his footsteps behind her and the sound of his quickened breathing.

In that short walk into the sitting-room she'd managed to compose herself, to have ready the answers to the questions she knew he'd start to fire at her, when all at once a hot dart of fire squeezed at her womb. Breathless with the impact, Kimberley clung on to the back of the nearest chair. Beads of sweat broke out on her forehead.

Harrison's eyes narrowed; he was by her side in an instant. 'What's happening?'

Another iron band constricted her; she panted the way she'd been taught. The sensation dominated her entire world, so that she was scarcely aware of the man who stood before her, his face creased with concern.

'I think—I think it's the baby,' she managed to get out. But it couldn't be! She couldn't be having the baby now—she *couldn't*. Not when she still had four weeks to go. She wrapped her hands tightly around her abdomen, glancing at her wristwatch as she did so. Time them, she remembered. Time the contractions.

He was really the last person in the world she should have wanted there, and yet, in reality, the sight of his broad, strong body made her feel ridiculously safe, and she could have wept, because his strength and dependability were nothing but an illusion.

He was staring at her very hard as he took in her pale, clammy face. 'What do you want me to do?' he fired out briskly.

'Ring the midwife. The number's on the pad. I need—— *Oh*!' she gasped. Another. And stronger this time. And only two minutes after the last.

For a moment he hesitated, moved over to take her by the shoulders, grey eyes searching her face, and then he said, 'Sit down,' and helped her gently down on to the sofa before going to telephone.

Harrison stood by the telephone, listening intently to the midwife. He glanced at his own wristwatch. 'Two minutes,' he said briefly into the mouthpiece. 'And they're regular.'

So he'd been timing them too, thought Kimberley, and then another wave hit her and she shifted restlessly on the sofa, the sweat now drying icily on her face.

Harrison was replacing the receiver. 'The ambulance is on its way. Tell me where your overnight bag is!'

'In the bedroom.' She closed her eyes as another hot, dark stab clutched at her.

Harrison returned moments later. His face was guarded as he crouched down beside her. 'Do you want me to call anyone for you?'

'Like who?' she enquired faintly.

'Like your mother?'

'No,' she whispered, from between dry lips. 'She—doesn't know.'

'I see,' he said grimly.

'Harrison...' Her voice tailed off.

'What?'

'You won't tell her? Please don't tell her!' she begged as the pain swamped her again.

'Tell her? Why should I? It's nothing to do with me.' His grey eyes were penetrating as he stared down at her. 'Is it, Kimberley?'

'No.' She shut her eyes, afraid that her fears and her feelings might show. He hadn't asked. Amazing. But the baby was early, and perhaps he... he... thought. Tears threatened to well at the bitter thought. Why should he suspect that she was having his baby? He probably thought that he was only one of a long line of lovers in her life.

Forcing herself, she opened her eyes and looked up at him. 'Can I have some water, please?'

He frowned. 'I don't know whether you should.'

'Why not?'

'Well, if they have to give you an anaes-thetic——'

'For God's sake!' Alarmed, Kimberley sat bolt-upright, her hair snaking wildly down her back. 'I'm only having a baby—why should they want to give me——?'

'Shh,' he soothed her. 'We'll compromise.' He disappeared into the kitchen and returned with a clean towel and a bowl of cool water, with which he proceeded to dampen her lips.

'Oh!' She smiled up into his eyes. 'That's good.'

He gave her a strange smile and nodded, but he didn't speak, just continued to dab at her dry lips every two seconds.

They heard the siren long before the ambulance screeched up outside the front door, and Kimberley tried and failed to stand up.

'Stay there!' ordered Harrison. 'They'll send a wheelchair for you.'

'Such a fuss,' she mumbled, until she discovered that the wheelchair was infinitely preferable to walking.

'She's going to be all right, isn't she?' demanded Harrison, and the ambulanceman gave him a reassuring smile.

'Don't worry, sir—she looks fit enough to me. In my experience it's always the father who goes to pieces! You'll have a healthy baby son or daughter before you know it, sir!'

She knew what conclusion they'd jumped to. She wanted to tell them that Harrison wasn't the father, but now they were putting a mask over her face, telling her to breathe deeply, and the sickly sweet smell of gas was making her feel disorientated, making the pain retreat, become bearable.

'Can you get in the back, please, sir?'

Harrison climbed in beside her, some dark and unfathomable emotion on his face as he stared down at her.

'What are you doing?' she asked in bewilderment.

'I'm coming with you,' he stated.

'Harrison——'

'You can't be on your own,' he said in a voice which brooked no argument. 'I'm staying.'

She stared up at that strong, beautiful face, found herself wanting to touch it, to tell him... Not just about the baby, to tell him that... She reached her hand out and he gripped it. 'Harrison,' she whispered, but then another contraction, stronger and more intense than any of the preceding ones, made her pupils dilate in pain, and the ambulanceman put a finger over his lips.

'Don't talk! Concentrate on your breathing,' he said urgently. 'And say a prayer that the traffic's quiet!'

The ambulance pulled away—the driver obviously had his foot down—and the journey all became a blur to Kimberley. She was aware of little other than the bands of contraction, which became fiercer and stronger and closer together. She was aware of gripping Harrison's hand, with her nails digging into his flesh so tightly that he should have winced, but he didn't wince, just gently smoothed the sweat-soaked strands of black hair which fell over her cheek from time to time. I must look absolutely awful, thought Kimberley fleetingly.

By the time they reached St Christopher's, Kimberley was past caring *what* she looked like, or even what was happening. They were bundling her on a stretcher and travelling upwards in a lift and then into a room which looked less like a ward than somebody's bedroom. It was all part of the new, relaxed policy towards birth, remembered Kimberley as Harrison helped lift her on to a flower-sprigged bed. She recognised one of the midwives she'd seen at her hospital appointments, who now began to examine her.

'Please,' Kimberley gasped. 'Can I have an epidural now?'

The midwife laughed. 'An epidural? Oh, heavens no, dear—it's far too late for that.'

'Too late?'

'Why, yes—the baby's on its way now. Keep breathing the way you've been taught, and any minute now I'm going to ask you to start pushing.'

Pain swamped her; someone wiped her brow and Kimberley looked up to see Harrison's darkly handsome face swimming into view.

'Harrison——' she said weakly, but he shook his head.

'Don't talk. Save your strength for the baby. It's all right—I'm here and I'm not leaving you.'

Oh, if only. The face swam away again. It was too late to tell him now. She felt a desire to push which consumed her... She saw the midwife's encouraging nod... Minutes later the baby was born and immediately gave a lusty cry.

'It's a girl!' said Harrison softly, bending his head to speak in her ear. 'A beautiful baby girl.'

And Kimberley burst into tears.

They laid the baby on her breast and Kimberley experienced the strangest, strongest sensation, of being physically exhausted and yet wonderfully, powerfully strong and triumphant.

'And Daddy can hold her in a minute,' smiled the midwife.

Kimberley said nothing, just stared down at the black little head which nestled against her. Too confusing to try to explain. Certainly not now.

'She's a fine healthy girl,' said the midwife. 'And a good weight, too—considering that she's early.' She smiled at Kimberley. 'Have you changed your mind about the adoption, now that you're back with the baby's daddy?'

The world spun on its axis.

Kimberley glanced up to find a pair of perceptive grey eyes, suddenly gone as cold as an arctic sky, boring into hers. He knows, she thought, with a sudden flash of insight. He knows he's the baby's father.

'Adoption?' he queried softly.

The midwife was beginning to look confused; perhaps things were not all they seemed with this striking-looking couple, she thought. Embarrassed, she turned away and began to wash her hands at the sink.

'Adoption?' he repeated, and there was a frozen look of rage on his face.

Words failed her. Literally. She gave a gulping speechless nod.

There was no way out. Not now. 'Yes,' she told him, lifting her chin defiantly. 'I intend to have the baby adopted.'

'I see,' he said, in a voice so sombre that Kimberley's skin turned to ice.

CHAPTER SEVEN

KIMBERLEY didn't know what she had expected to
happen—but what she had *not* expected was that
cold and terse little nod he gave her.

'I'll let you get some rest now,' he said abruptly.
'I'll be back later.'

It was like a sentence of death hanging over her
head. Kimberley fed the baby, and they both slept.
They gave her a cup of strong tea and a marmalade
sandwich, then she had a wash, and the staff nurse
washed and brushed her hair for her.

'Got to look pretty for your boyfriend,' she said
to Kimberley confidingly. 'I can't keep the student
nurses away—they're dying to see him again. What
a hunk—are there any more like him at home?'

Kimberley tried to smile, and failed. Her lip
wobbled precariously and the staff nurse nodded
understandingly.

'Feeling a bit blue, are we? Don't worry, dear.'
She plumped the four pillows into shape behind
Kimberley's back. 'It's quite normal to feel like that
afterwards.' She beamed down at the sleeping
infant. 'Decided what to call her yet, have you?'

Kimberley swallowed. She had discussed this with
her doctor. Apparently it didn't matter *what* name
she called her baby, because the adoptive parents
would probably change it. She stared down at the
crib. So, even though she might call her Georgia or

100

Alicia—two names she liked very much—her daughter might instead grow up as an Anne or a Mary.

She must have dozed off, because when she awoke it was to find Harrison there, at the end of the bed. He was studying the child intently, an expression of rapt preoccupation on his face, but he seemed to sense that Kimberley's eyes had opened, for he glanced up immediately and a coldly indifferent look chilled his face.

'Harrison——' she began, but he stopped her with one decisive shake of his dark head, an expression of distaste curving his mouth scornfully.

'Save it.' He spoke tersely. 'I don't want any more of your lies. She's mine, isn't she?'

'Harrison——'

'*Isn't* she?'

Dispiritedly Kimberley sank back against the pillows. 'Yes. She's yours.'

It was as though her spoken admission, even though he had known it to be a fact, had shocked him to the core. He stared first at Kimberley—and the look of naked pain and anger and hatred in his eyes scorched her to the very core—then shook his head very slowly from side to side, as though he couldn't really take it in.

'But you knew all along, didn't you?' she asked weakly. 'Why didn't you say something?'

His mouth became a grim, harsh line. 'You may have a low opinion of me, Kimberley, but I'm not in the habit of debating paternity when a woman is in labour.' A muscle began to work furiously beneath one perfect cheekbone. 'Just tell me,' he said,

in a strange, gritty voice, 'tell me that you aren't
planning to have her adopted.'

She heard the plea in his voice, and she couldn't
lie to him—but neither could she prevent her voice
from shaking. 'I—yes,' she managed. 'Yes, I am.'

The look he gave her was one of pure contempt.

'My God,' he whispered in disbelief. 'I thought
that my opinion of you couldn't possibly sink any
lower, but I was wrong. It was bad enough when
you traded my brother in because you fancied
making a quick buck. But this...' He shook his
head. '*This* defies all comparison. What right did
you have, Kimberley, to deny me all knowledge of
the fact that I was going to have a child? Have a
child.' And his face softened marginally as his eyes
strayed to the snuffling infant.

Kimberley was fighting for her life—her sanity.
'What *right*?' she demanded, not caring who heard
her. 'You forfeited any *right* when you offered me
that one night! A quick roll in the hay doesn't
automatically guarantee your *rights*! If you recall,
you couldn't wait to make sure that I'd actually
used some contraception—and I'm ashamed to say
that even the thought of it never occurred to
me——'

'Because you were so hot for me,' he said
insultingly.

She knew that his need to wound her was deep,
and that it stemmed from discovering that she had
kept the secret of his paternity from him, but
knowing that didn't stop it hurting. 'Yes, I was
"hot" for you—as you so delightfully put it. I'm

sure that's nothing new, Harrison. You're pretty good in bed.'

He gave an angry snarl, his eyes sparked fire, but then, as if he was remembering just where they were, and that Kimberley had given birth less than four hours ago, he stopped himself from responding with what was obviously a huge effort.

'Why *should* I have saddled you with a baby from what was never supposed to be anything more than a one-night stand?'

He flinched, a muscle working frantically in his cheek. 'You too,' he answered coldly, 'have such a delightful way with words.'

She felt deflated. What was the point of all this?

'May I hold her?' he asked suddenly.

Kimberley nodded, feeling tears prick at the back of her eyes as she watched him bend down and cradle the tiny bundle, before lifting her up to lie her on his shoulder, placing the large and soft shawl tenderly around her shoulders.

He stood like that for a moment, completely unconscious of the striking picture he made, just gently rocking back and forth on his heels, and the baby gave a sigh. He was so tall, so strong—so powerfully masculine—and yet he was as gentle as a kitten with the baby. A student nurse stuck her head round the door and almost swooned, but his eyes narrowed by a fraction, he gave the tiniest shake of his head, and the nurse took the hint and scuttled off.

'But the end result is the same,' he said heavily, his eyes going reluctantly to Kimberley's, and she blinked away the glittering tears which sparkled at the ice-blue depths. 'What have you decided to call her?'

'Can't we talk about this some other time?' she pleaded.

He shook his head. 'I've certainly no wish to tire you out. I won't keep you long, and the whole business will be kept on a completely impartial basis.'

What on earth was he talking about?

'But I have to go abroad for a few days,' he continued, 'and we must get a few things settled before I go. Like her name.' And he smiled into the soft, downy black head.

Kimberley felt panicked. She had to tell him. She took a deep breath. 'It doesn't really matter what I'm going to call her,' she reminded him gently. 'Because I'm going to have her adopted.'

There was a strange, frightening look on his face as he enunciated the single word. 'Why?'

'Because I don't feel it would be fair—to keep her——'

'Fair to whom?' he interrupted coldly. 'To you— or to her?'

Kimberley tried to explain. 'What chance would she have? Brought up by a single mother who has to go out to work to support her? I'd have to work late some nights—what then? Stuck at some child-minder's—her never seeing me, me never seeing her. And when I did I'd be too tired and——'

'You selfish little liar! How dare you even consider it?'

Kimberley exploded with rage. 'How dare *you*?' she demanded. 'You talk about rights—what *right* do you have as a man to try and take some ridiculously moral stance on what I should do? If you must know, I thought I *was* doing the right thing by the baby. I thought two parents were better than one——'

'But she *has* two parents,' he pointed out.

Kimberley stared at him. 'Just what are you suggesting?'

'I'm not suggesting anything at the moment, I'm merely stating a fact. But one thing is certain, Kimberley—I will not have my daughter put up for adoption, and I'll fight you through every court in the land to stop you.'

There was a whimpering at his shoulder, which rapidly gave way to a shrill shriek emitted by the widest mouth on such a tiny little creature that Kimberley could imagine.

She held her arms out. 'Give her to me.'

The momentary hesitation on his face nearly killed her, but then he handed the baby over reluctantly, frowning slightly as he watched her suckle Kimberley immediately—the shriek becoming a blissful glug as the baby greedily drank the milk.

Harrison moved towards the bed. Towering over it, he was at an advantage, and his grey eyes burned their ice-fire into hers. 'I have to go abroad for a few days—there's nothing I can do about it.'

'It's of no concern to me.'

He shook his head. 'Oh, but it is, Kimberley,' he contradicted her. 'It concerns you very much. Don't even attempt to give the baby up. I shall instruct my lawyers to act for me at once—and don't think it's an idle boast when I tell you that you'll have no case against me.'

'Case?' What was he talking about? 'Just what are you planning to do?'

'I'll adopt her myself—that's my plan. As you don't want her. And one other thing—I want us to agree on a name before I go. I'm fed up with calling her "she" already.' There was a pause. 'Had you any names in mind?'

'Why consult *me*?' she whispered brokenly. 'I'm only her mother.'

'And mothers fight to *keep* their children,' he snarled. 'Not give them away.'

Kimberley bit her lip, not trusting herself to say anything.

'So. Names?'

'I like Georgia,' she said reluctantly. 'Or Alicia.'

'I like Georgia, too,' he said surprisingly. 'I like it very much.' The baby finished feeding and he was staring down at her, entranced. Quite instinctively Kimberley held her out to him.

Without being told, he winded her and changed her nappy; he was brilliant for a beginner, Kimberley conceded, then she watched as he laid her carefully down in her crib and tucked the shawl round her.

'Goodbye, sweet little Georgia,' he said softly, and as he straightened from planting a kiss on the soft little cheek he said something else softly, too. Very softly—but Kimberley heard it. 'Let's hope you don't grow up to be a lying little cheat like your mother.'

And he walked out of the room without a backward glance, leaving Kimberley shaken and close to tears, and on the brink of a truth which had nagged at her and refused to leave her since the first time Georgia had lain on her breast and a tiny little hand had curled itself tightly around her finger.

Her words had been empty, her thoughts wishful.

She would move heaven and earth to keep her baby.

CHAPTER EIGHT

KIMBERLEY and Georgia stayed in the hospital for five days. They told her that this was usual for first-time mothers, particularly as the baby had been early.

Kimberley had sent James out with a fortune to spend on baby clothes, delighting in the tiny garments he had brought back. She'd have to buy a pram, she knew, and a cot—countless things—but she'd wait until she was discharged and then go choose them herself.

Two days after Harrison left for France a giant pink teddy bear had arrived, with a card saying, 'To the most beautiful baby in the world. With love from Daddy'. And just the sight of it had filled Kimberley with an inexplicable fear.

She was packing her suitcase to go home when he walked into the room. She was crouched over her suitcase wearing a broderie anglaise cotton shirt, which buttoned down the front so that she could breastfeed, and it came to mid-thigh. She saw the reluctant darkening of his eyes as his glance roved over her semi-clothed state and felt colour scorch her cheeks as she registered his physical presence, the impact he always made on her. Her breasts tingled, and she felt as though her body had completely betrayed her—for surely it wasn't normal to ache and hunger for a man when you'd only just had his baby?

Over the past five days she'd had time to reflect on her behaviour, deciding that she had been wrong and cowardly not to tell him. Yet it had seemed the only thing to do at the time, and it was now far too late to make amends.

But sooner rather than later he was going to find out that she had no intention of letting Georgia be adopted, and if he was going to demand access, which she was certain he was going to do, then it would be infinitely preferable if their relationship was polite and civilised rather than as tempestuous as it had been up until now.

'Hello,' she said.

He stared at her swiftly, seeming to gauge her mood. 'Hello.' He glanced over at the crib. 'How is she?'

Kimberley smiled. 'Just perfect—though I'm biased, of course! She's——'

'I have a car waiting,' he said abruptly.

Kimberley blinked. 'What for?'

'To take you home, of course—or did you imagine that I would have you call a cab?'

Kimberley held her chin up—he was making it sound as though she had no one in the world to care about her. 'As a matter of fact, James is on his way to collect me.'

The face blackened. 'Then he'll have a wasted journey, won't he?' he snarled.

'Meaning?'

'You're coming with me, Kimberley—and that's that. Now, would you mind getting dressed?'

Feeling cornered, she gave a nod, biting her lip as she did so. She mustn't keep antagonising him; he would make a cruel adversary. 'Would you mind turning your back?' she asked stiffly.

'A little late in the day for modesty, wouldn't you say?' came his harsh rejoinder, but he did as she asked, and Kimberley silently put on a lemon silk shirt and a grey pleated skirt with trembling fingers, amazed that the waistband of the skirt wasn't in the least bit tight.

'You can turn around again now,' she told him.

He narrowed his grey eyes as he watched her pull the brush through the thick black silk of her hair, seemingly fascinated by the movement as it spilled glossily down over her breasts.

A muscle worked in his cheek as he gestured towards the baby. 'Do you want to carry her, or shall I?'

And then, remembering the tender way with which he'd handled the baby, she managed a smile. 'You can carry her if you like.'

His mouth twisted; she was becoming used to that critical curve. 'Of course,' he mocked.

The nurses came in, an absolute gaggle of them, to say goodbye and to thank Harrison. Apparently he had not only left them chocolates, champagne, fruit and flowers, but had stuck a very hefty cheque into the Nurses' Benevolent Fund, with instructions that they use it for their Christmas dance. Whereupon he had immediately been invited to be guest of honour!

Kimberley watched all the laughing interaction with a growing uneasiness which she was reluctantly beginning to recognise as jealousy.

Outside she did not see the ridiculously expensive black car, but instead a discreetly gleaming green Bentley, complete with a chauffeur who held open the back door, and Kimberley climbed in, followed by Harrison holding on to Georgia.

There was a tiny baby-seat in place, and Harrison gently clipped the baby in.

Kimberley grew confused. 'Your car is different. I thought you drove a black car.'

'Not exclusively. This is one of several I own.'

'And I suppose they all have baby-seats?'

'The ones which aren't sports models do. Now. I had them installed last week—it seemed practical.'

Kimberley swallowed. He'd talked about adopting Georgia, but that had been before—before she'd decided that she couldn't let her baby go. 'Harrison——'

He frowned. 'Let's not begin what is obviously going to be a difficult conversation in the car, Kimberley. In the circumstances, I feel it is more prudent to wait until we get home.'

'Prudent?' she demanded, angry at being spoken to in that admonitory manner, but even angrier at the way he was fast taking the upper hand. She turned her face to stare sightlessly out of the window—anything was better than having to be made aware of that daunting physical presence. And she was supposed to be adopting a civilised attitude towards him, she reminded herself. She might find it difficult, but she really ought to try. 'It's very kind of you to give us a lift home,' she said.

'My pleasure,' he answered, in a tone which made mockery of his words.

But the car was going nowhere near Hampstead. Instead she started to recognise signs for the south-west. 'Where are we going?' she asked suddenly.

'To Kew.'

'Why Kew?'

'It's where I live.'

'Harrison—I want to go home.'

'And that, too, is something we must discuss. But not now.'

He was quite emphatic in his refusal to say anything further, and he didn't utter another word until the car had drawn up outside some wrought-iron railings in front of an enormous double-fronted house which stood in its own walled garden.

As he walked alongside her, carrying Georgia, she became aware that the garden was a scented paradise—there were stocks and honeysuckle, tobacco plants and sweet roses, and, with the mellow brick of the wall acting as a backdrop, tall delphiniums and hollyhocks, too. She liked it; she liked it very much. Did he garden, or did someone do it for him? But even if he did employ a gardener he surely must have had some input in the creation of this country garden right in the middle of the city? Ironic, really. How little she really knew about the father of her child.

She followed him inside, but by this time she wasn't taking very much in—only that the ceilings were high and the rooms large and well-proportioned. In the spacious wood-panelled entrance hall stood a top-of-the-range pram, with a flaxen-haired doll smiling inanely at them from its depths.

Panic mounting, Kimberley turned to him. 'What on earth is going on, Harrison? Why have you brought me here? And why are all these baby things lying around?'

He gave her a chilly smile. 'I brought the baby here because there was nothing for her at your house. Not a single item of clothing, not even a cot for her to sleep in. But then, I suppose as you had planned to hand her over to someone else just as soon as you could——'

Past feeling the pain of his censure, Kimberley caught his arm. 'I want to explain to you——'

'Frankly, I'm not interested in your explanations, but I will give you a chance to speak. After we get Georgia settled. She is, after all,' he emphasised, 'the important one.' But the look on his face suggested that she thought otherwise. And who could blame him? thought Kimberley wildly, seeing her actions through his eyes for the first time.

And waiting for them in the drawing-room was a girl of around twenty-three, with a cap of gleaming blonde hair surrounding a serene and smiling face. She was dressed in a brown and white uniform which stirred some vague memory in Kimberley's mind.

'Hello, Sarah,' smiled Harrison. 'We've brought the baby home, and I'd like you to meet Kimberley Ryan, her mother.'

Kimberley's heart gave a great leap of alarm and she looked up at Harrison, a question in her eyes.

'This is Sarah Hansford,' he said in a neutral voice. 'Who is to be Georgia's nanny.'

Georgia's nanny!

'I'm pleased to meet you,' said Sarah, and held out her hand, but her pale eyes were not on Kimberley, or on Georgia, instead they were fixed very firmly and adoringly on Harrison.

Kimberley felt faint. How could he have appointed a nanny without consulting her? 'And is this your first job, Sarah?' she probed.

Sarah's eyes glinted, and she almost seemed to inflate herself before their eyes. 'Oh, no. I worked for a member of the royal family until I accepted Mr Nash's offer of a job.'

'I see.' Kimberley felt as though the world around her was going mad, as if she'd somehow managed to lose control of her own destiny.

'I'd like to talk to you, please, Harrison. Alone,' she added pointedly. 'I've fed Georgia, Sarah—I think you'll find she's ready for her bath before bedtime. Then I'll come up and settle her down for the night.'

Sarah took Georgia into her arms, and Kimberley couldn't fault the way she held the baby. But her next words filled her once more with an inexplicable dread. 'Oh, don't you worry about a thing, Miss Ryan. I'd prefer to adopt my own routine, if you don't mind. Nanny knows *best*—doesn't she, Georgia?'

Kimberley let her go. There was too much which needed to be sorted out. But once they had disappeared she turned to Harrison. 'Who is this girl?' she hissed as she watched Sarah carry the baby upstairs. 'I don't know her from Adam.'

'She comes highly recommended. She looked after a friend of mine's children for several years.'

Was he talking about the royal? wondered Kimberley faintly.

'She's excellent,' he continued. 'Firm, kind, with the sort of old-fashioned methods of child-rearing which I thoroughly approve of.'

He had thought everything through, Kimberley realised. With as much detail as a military campaign. 'And which methods are they?'

He shrugged. 'Regular meals, regular bedtimes. Firm handling with limitless love. How does that sound?'

'And how many other staff do you have?' she asked, imagining a legion of maids suddenly appearing.

'Just someone to clean and to garden, and Mrs Caithness prepares the food—although I use a firm of caterers for large functions, of course. But that doesn't really concern you, does it, Kimberley? I mean, it's not as though you're staying.'

Kimberley's head swam. 'Could we please talk now?' she asked desperately.

'Sure.'

'Don't you think that you ought to have consulted me about something as important as hiring a nanny?'

'Frankly, I didn't think that you'd be particularly concerned about it either way,' he said sardonically.

'Well, I w-would,' she stumbled, then closed her eyes quickly, lest he see the tears that glittered there.

But if he didn't see the tears then the tremor in her voice alerted him, made him look up sharply. He studied her face very closely for a long moment, and when he spoke his voice was quite gentle. 'You're very pale. Why don't you make yourself comfortable and we can talk?' He gestured towards a sofa. 'Would you like some wine?'

She would have loved some, but had grown so used to avoiding alcohol, avoiding smoke and smokers, and considering all the other responsibilities of pregnancy, that it was going to take a little time for her to relinquish them. 'I'd love some. But I wonder would a glass be OK—with me feeding Georgia?' she asked automatically.

Another quick glance, definitely tinged with surprise this time—as though he was taken aback at her solicitude. He looked as though he was on the brink of smiling, then appeared to change his mind. 'I'm sure that one glass won't hurt. Wait here while I fetch some.'

He left the room and reappeared moments later, carrying a bottle and two crystal goblets. There was silence as he opened it, and she found herself observing him unobtrusively while pretending to study a superb water-colour which hung over the fireplace.

He looked so tense, his face so grave and unsmiling. She found herself remembering that night of love, the rapture on his face when he'd told her that she was beautiful, and she'd given him that cold and, she'd thought, clever little reply. Another wall she'd built around herself.

Since the moment she'd met him she'd been constructing walls to protect her from being hurt by him. And every one of her actions had been badly misconstrued by him. She had always wanted him to think the worst of her, and he did. But she found herself wanting to defend herself on something as important as this—not so that he would think well of her, but so that he would trust her to bring up their child properly.

And it was therefore vital that she convince him she had *thought* that she had acted in Georgia's best interests in trying to conceal her from him. For it seemed the most awful kind of crime that a man— and not just any man—that Harrison should imagine that she had cared nothing for the child which had grown within her.

'Here.' He interrupted her reverie, handed her a glass of red wine and motioned for her to sit down. She perched down on the sofa but he remained standing, his face unreadable as he started to speak.

'I told you that I intended speaking to my lawyers, and now I have. They——' he began, but Kimberley began to tremble and she quickly put the glass of wine down on the small table. Still it slopped over the side, her hand was shaking so much.

'Please, Harrison, before you say anything more about lawyers, I want you to know that I've had a good chance to think things through, and—well, the point is that things have changed, or rather *I've* changed. And I don't want Georgia to be adopted.'

There was silence. He sipped his drink. 'I see,'
was all he said for a moment or two. He took
another sip of wine, before studying her with those
clear grey eyes. 'And what brought all this on—
this sudden change of heart? Or is it simply to
prevent me from having her?'

Surely he knew? And hadn't he felt it too—that
overpowering surge of emotion at holding a child
that you'd created in your arms? 'I just—didn't
know that I'd feel this way about her. I think that
I must have been very slightly mad to think I'd ever
be able to give her up for adoption,' she finished
quietly.

A slight inclination of the dark, elegant head was
the only indication that he'd heard her softly spoken
words. 'And just what are you proposing to do?
How will you manage?'

'I've got to speak to James, see if he'll let me go
back to work part-time——'

'And if he doesn't?'

'I'm kind of depending on him saying yes, but
if he doesn't—well, then I'll have to rethink. But
I'm young—adaptable. I've got a brain in my head.
I'll take whatever work comes along to support us.
It might be a bit of a struggle, but I'm prepared
for that.'

'And isn't that the very scenario which turned
you against single parenthood in the first place?'

Kimberley swallowed. 'You know it is. Perhaps
now you'll realise that I *was* thinking of the baby's
best interests. This way will be harder financially,
but emotionally—there really is no alternative. Now
I've got her—I can't let her go.'

He nodded his head, as if considering what she'd said. 'And what about me?'

She knew immediately what he meant. 'Oh, I have no intention of denying you access,' she told him quickly.

'That's *terribly* generous of you,' he said sardonically. 'What kind of access did you have in mind?'

'The usual,' she said bluntly.

'The *usual*?' he bit back. 'And what's that? Every other weekend? A few weeks in the summer?'

'I'm prepared to be more generous than that——' she began.

'Well, let me tell you that I am *not* prepared to accept any grudging bits of largesse you may condescend to bestow on me. If you had gone through with your plan to give her up for adoption, I would—as I told you—have been perfectly agreeable to adopting her myself.'

'But now I'm not going to do that, am I?'

'No. And, while I am not cynical enough to try and deprive a child of her mother, neither do I intend to be a part-time father. Which leaves us only one alternative.'

'Which is?'

'That she has two parents.'

A frown creased her forehead. 'But how——?'

'There's only one way.' He said it without expression. 'That you marry me.'

Kimberley stared at him. 'You cannot be serious.'

He reached forward, tipped some more of the wine into his glass, then came and sat down beside her, leaning back against the sofa and sipping his wine, watching her coolly, as though he had not just dropped a bombshell. 'Oh, but that's where you're wrong, Kimberley.' He smiled. 'I am. Deadly serious.'

'But—men don't have to marry women for that reason any more. Not these days.'

'I know they don't. But perhaps sometimes they should. Particularly in our case. Imagine the hurt we're going to cause our families, just for starters. Your mother has yet to find out that you have a child, and she is bound to want to know who the father is. Now, while you might be tempted to tell her yet another lie——'

'I——' She tried to interrupt, but he shook his head and refused to let her.

'I have no intention of letting Georgia's paternity remain a secret,' he continued, unperturbed. 'As I also have no intention of becoming a father on the very part-time basis which you wish to bestow on me. I want to be *involved* in her life. I want her to have stability—both emotional *and* financial—and I can provide that.'

Kimberley shook her head sorrowfully. 'But you seem to be forgetting our mutual antipathy and distrust—do you think that's going to provide much stability?'

His eyes glittered. 'That depends on how we set this marriage up.'

He was unbelievable! 'You mean, like setting a company up?'

'Why not? Any institution works best within a framework—provided that framework is not too constricting.'

'And what "framework" did you have in mind for our marriage?' she asked quietly.

'You shall have all the independence you require. The best nannies, staff—you can start back to work just as soon as you like.'

'That sounds exceedingly generous, Harrison. And just what would you get out of it?'

'I would expect you to play the corporate wife— within limits, naturally. But you would be required to host dinners, and weekends occasionally, at whichever house I happen to be staying in. There will be some travel—but that can be tailored to suit the needs of your career. What I require most, of course, is the opportunity to be a hands-on father, and marriage is the most sensible way for me to accomplish that.'

There was a subject which he had completely ignored, of course. Kimberley struggled to keep her voice steady as she asked the question. 'And is that it?'

'*It?*' He gave a cruel and suddenly ruthless smile, as though he'd guessed exactly what was on her mind. 'Could you be a little more specific?'

'You know exactly what I mean!' she said bitterly, the colour flooding her pale face.

'Do I?' he murmured, moving closer as with one finger he outlined each of her dark, bold eyebrows, as though he'd been painting them.

'Ye-es,' she said shakily, wishing that he wouldn't do that, and yet making no attempt to stop him because her skin was rejoicing in the sensual caress of his touch. Touch was dangerous. The slightest brush of his fingertip sent little shivers of sensation rippling from the point of contact to every single nerve-ending in her body.

'You have,' he murmured, 'such exceptionally fine eyebrows—so strong and so exquisitely shaped. Pre-Raphaelite, in fact. Almost as beautifully shaped as your lips, which are just crying out— aren't they, Kimberley,' he whispered, 'to be kissed?'

The temptation was overpowering; his face was so close, his mouth was so close...so very temptingly close. She stared into those eyes, now smoky with passion, with want, with need, and he must have read her own helpless surrender, for he bent his head to take her mouth softly in a kiss.

Kimberley's eyes fluttered to a close as she succumbed to that sweet, heady sensation, the melting flood of desire flooding her veins immediately, kickstarting her senses into glorious, forgotten life. And what had started as pliant submission vanished as she put her arms around his broad shoulders and kissed him back, with a hunger of such raw and sensual depth that she began to tremble uncontrollably.

He felt her give-away, blatant response to his kiss and he muttered something inaudible against her mouth and began to kiss her, as though her instant and unhidden hunger had driven him over the edge of reason and towards insanity, as if the cool, calculating man of a few moments ago had been vanquished forever.

His mouth was now on the slim, pale column of her neck, and he was pushing the thick silken ropes of black hair back over her shoulders impatiently, as if he wanted to expose more flesh. And more. He began to undo the buttons of her lemon shirt, each one slipping aside easily so that it slithered open, revealing her lush and swollen breasts. She watched while his eyes darkened, saw him urgently unclip the bra, barely waiting until her breasts came tumbling out, free and unfettered, before his head swooped to take one swollen and erect nipple possessively into the hot, passionate cavern of his mouth.

Kimberley almost fainted with pleasure, a small gasp escaping her lips, and he released her breast at once, looking up at her, his eyes hopelessly dazed.

'Am I hurting you?'

She shook her head; never in his arms could he hurt her—in that place he offered only pleasure of untold delight. 'Oh, no.'

'Do you like it?' he murmured. 'Shall I do it again?'

'Yes.'

'Like this?' he whispered as his mouth closed over the pointed peak once more.

'Just like that.' She made the throaty assertion without thinking. 'Oh, *yes*,' she breathed ecstatically. She just couldn't stop herself. Later she might despise herself, but for the moment she was at the mercy of the sweet command he seemed to exert over her body, and at the mercy of her feelings for him—her love and her need.

For she loved Harrison; she had loved him from the first moment he had taken her into his arms, and despite all her protestations that love had never really diminished. She had lain with him and borne his child, and right now—powerful and primitive— came the sweeping desire from deep within her to have this man who had impregnated her, to have him fill her with his need once more.

His mouth tugged and suckled at her again, and the dizzy darts of pleasure swam through her veins as thick and sweet as honey.

'Touch me,' he whispered against her breast. 'Kimberley. Touch me.'

The almost helpless appeal in his voice turned her on unbearably—and she had done this to him. She had the power to disintegrate that cool exterior, that hard ruthlessness he had demonstrated so often, and turn him into this man who was going out of his mind for her.

She touched his chest lightly, touched the nipples through his shirt, and he moved his hand up her leg beneath her skirt, his fingers running luxuriously around the lacy rim of her stocking-top.

'Now touch me as I'm going to touch you,' he ordered in a velvety whisper.

And she did. She let her hand stray down to find his hardness. And, oh, yes—he wanted her. He *really* wanted her. She moved her hips, inviting him to touch her where he'd promised, but instead he moved to lie on top of her, shaking his head, barely able to speak coherently.

'Not here. We'd better go upstairs to bed. Sarah might—— '

Sarah? The unfamiliar name darted into the mists of Kimberley's befuddled mind, and just the mention of the nanny's name brought the uneasy situation back into sharp and distressing reality. She moved away, wriggling out from beneath him, and positioned herself at the end of the sofa, her face averted, burning with shame, afraid to look at him until she had her desire for him under control. Because she was in such a highly volatile state that one look from him and she would go under yet again.

She fumbled with her bra.

'Can I help?' There was hateful amusement in his voice, and this infuriated her more than anything. Any other man would have been angry; *she* was angry—and so het up that it hurt. Whereas he had himself firmly under control. She didn't bother to reply, just reclipped her bra and rebuttoned her shirt calmly, as though that were the kind of thing she did regularly.

'Now,' he murmured, 'just what were we talking about? Remind me.'

'Don't be obtuse, Harrison,' she bit back, goaded by his attitude.

He clapped his hand on to his forehead in mock brainwave. 'Eureka! I've remembered—we were debating the nebulous subject of "it". By "it",' he continued, still in that hateful, mocking voice, 'I assume you want to know whether I will require you in my bed at night? Well, I think we've just demonstrated very effectively what the answer to that is.'

She felt like slapping him in the face as hard as she possibly could, but she was in no position to play the shrinking violet, whose reputation he had besmirched with his words.

But he wouldn't talk to her as though she were ... as though ... 'Don't you dare speak to me as though I'm some kind of whore, Harrison. I won't tolerate it.'

He laughed then, but it was a bitter, empty laugh. 'No? But I thought you had your price for everything, Kimberley—or perhaps you prefer to deny that, with the benefit of hindsight?'

She gave a heavy sigh as she remembered what she'd done. Oh, the impetuous behaviour of youth. A crazy stone thrown into the pond, and still the ripples reverberated down through the years. 'You're referring to the money you gave me to stay away from Duncan, I suppose?'

'That was, as I recall, the *only* time I offered you money. And rather a lot of it, too.'

The tension showed in the brittleness of her laugh. 'If only you knew the truth about why I accepted that money, Harrison!'

'Oh, I'd love to. Try me.'

'You'd never believe it in a million years ...'

'Try me?' he invited again.

She shook her head. She was weak enough, and if he ever found out about her unrequited love for him it would make her weaker still. How he would play with her if he had any idea of the foolish love she'd harboured for him over all these years. She wondered whether he would ever forgive her for saying that she wanted Georgia adopted. She very much doubted it. And imagine how sweet he could make his revenge if he suspected the true depth of her emotional attachment to him.

'So we still haven't settled the subject of conjugal rights,' he persisted. 'But I'd like to reassure you that it's entirely up to you. I certainly shan't force you.' But the mocking tone spoke for itself—I wouldn't need to! 'Personally,' he continued, 'I would like to make it a marriage in the complete sense of the word.' And his eyes glittered like a stormy sea, sparkling with sexual anticipation, and she had to steel herself not to respond to their compelling light.

Because it could never be a 'complete' marriage, she thought sadly. Complete marriages meant that there was love, too—and there was no love between her and Harrison. None on his side, anyway—and wouldn't it grind away at her self-respect if she submitted to him? Knowing that she was nothing but a body he found irresistible—and for how long?

'However,' he continued, 'I can quite understand if you find the idea of sleeping with me distasteful. If, for example, you require a little more *variety* in your sex-life than I can provide. But if that's the case, my dear Kimberley, then count me out. I have to tell you that I will not share you. I am not——' his eyes glittered again, but this time with menace, with an underlying threat '—a sharing kind of man. All I would ask is that you be discreet—I won't have our daughter's name sullied by her schoolfriends knowing that her mother is a tramp.'

Kimberley swallowed the bile which had risen in

her throat. His regard for her really could sink no lower than it was at the moment.

'Your answer, my dear?' he asked mockingly.

She lifted her small chin proudly. 'You mean, to your very sweetly couched proposal?' she mocked him back.

'The very same,' he agreed gravely.

'It sounds worse than hell.'

'But that depends on your perception, surely?'

'And what's the alternative?' She twisted her hands together in her lap. 'To this farce of a marriage?'

There was a cruel smile. 'No alternative. Leastways, not one which you would find acceptable. If you refuse me, then we go to court and we have one hell of a custody battle on our hands. The costs,' he mused, with deliberate emphasis, 'could be astronomical. Do you think that you could afford to pay them, Kimberley?'

He knew she couldn't. He had her in every which way he could—and he knew that, too.

She stared angrily into the stormy grey eyes.

Some day, she vowed, Harrison Nash would live to regret what he was forcing her into.

CHAPTER NINE

'OH, KIMBERLEY, darling,' said Mrs Ryan wistfully. 'You look absolutely *beautiful*!'

'Do I?' Kimberley stared into the full-length mirror of her mother's bedroom to see a stranger, who looked exactly like her, all dressed up in her bridal finery.

'Mmm. Quite radiant—I can't wait to see Harrison's face!'

I can, thought Kimberley gloomily. The only thing I'm likely to see on Harrison's face is lust. Or contempt. Sometimes, in fact, she was cheered even to see *that*. At least it meant he was reacting to her with his mind rather than just his body.

In the past seven days since she'd been living with him—well, it wasn't exactly living *with* him, more like co-existing separately in the same house—she had barely seen him. He had been working all the hours that God sent. He played for an hour with Georgia early in the morning before he left for work, while Kimberley was still in bed, returning late in the evening, by which time she'd fallen back into bed, exhausted. But at least, she supposed, that cut down on the row situation.

She had been left alone with Georgia and the dreaded Sarah. Sarah who seemed to eat away at her self-confidence, telling her that everything she did for Georgia was wrong.

Her prim little face would light up with delight as she imparted yet another snippet. 'Oh, *no*, Miss Ryan——' she never missed an opportunity to rub in Kimberley's single status '—we shouldn't breastfeed on *demand*! Baby will start to rule the roost, won't she? And that isn't good for her. Routine—that's what babies like. Now, why don't you let me bath her, while you go and put your feet up?'

Kimberley could have screamed, if she'd had the energy to scream, but Georgia was a fractious baby at night, waking several times regularly. This, too, was Kimberley's fault, according to Sarah, because she didn't give Georgia enough 'firm handling'.

It was all very well having a nanny, thought Kimberley wearily one night, as she padded bare-footed from her bedroom to the nursery next door, but they didn't give a hand during the small hours of the morning, when you were so tired you felt like dropping. She had tried to catch up on sleep during the day, but that was when sleep stubbornly refused to come, her mind so bound up with the situation she was in, with wondering why Harrison came in so late every evening, whether the fact that she had not taken him up on his offer to share his bedroom had anything to do with it.

Well, at least Sarah wouldn't be able to look down her nose at her for being an unmarried mother any more, because today she and Harrison were getting married, and in some considerable style, too.

Kimberley had thought it only appropriate—what with Georgia and all—to have a quick ceremony in a register office somewhere in London.

'And I suppose you'd like to pick up a couple of witnesses off the street?' Harrison had snarled. 'Just to *really* devalue it!'

She had tried to be reasonable. 'Well, it's not as though either of us are doing it because we *want* to, is it?'

And a funny little cold expression had creased the handsome face. 'No, of course it isn't, Kimberley.'

He had argued that she had denied her mother her pregnancy, and that being an only child she ought to allow her to participate in the wedding. 'And I know my mother would like to watch us get married,' he had added. 'My brother and Caroline, too.'

Now that had made her feel odd. 'OK,' she'd agreed. 'You obviously want to get married near Woolton.'

'*In* Woolton,' he contradicted.

'But the nearest register office is in——'

'I don't want to get married in a register office, Kimberley,' he had said. 'I want us to get married in a church. The church at Woolton.' He must have seen her disbelieving expression. 'For Georgia,' he had added.

Of course. He would move mountains for that child. If only... She blocked the thought as she stared at her wedding ensemble. There were to be no 'if only's in her life, and the sooner she accepted that, the better.

She had refused point-blank to get married in white—not with a two-week-old baby. Her mother had talked her into cream, however—and if she had only known it, the cream silk brought out the faint roses in her cheeks and warmed her pale skin where white would have drained it.

It was a simple dress, with a scoop neck and cap sleeves, and it came to just above the knee. She wore cream court shoes and a cream hat. The hat was her one big expense and her one frivolity, and it had cost more than the dress and shoes put together! It was a jaunty top hat in cream, from which floated a shoulder-length piece of tulle. She wore her shiny black hair pulled back from her face in a soft pleat, and the stark simplicity of the style suited her.

'You look so young,' said her mother wistfully. 'And so innocent.'

'Hardly innocent,' responded Kimberley drily. 'Not with a two-week-old baby!'

'Little treasure!' said Mrs Ryan fiercely. 'And don't you worry about that! Nearly everyone does it this way round these days. It's how you feel about each other that matters.'

Kimberley paused in the process of applying a light coat of pink lipstick. She couldn't let her mother carry on living in cloud-cuckoo-land about her and Harrison; she really couldn't. 'Mother— about me and Harrison——'

'I'm so lucky,' her mother almost crooned. 'To have him for a son-in-law. I really *like* him.' Her still exceptionally fine blue eyes sparkled with merriment. 'And I always suspected that there was something going on between the two of you—so did his mother. Especially after the party at their house. That's why I went to him to find out why you hadn't been in touch. Of course, I can't say that it wasn't a *shock* to find out that it was because you were pregnant, but still . . . All's well that ends well.'

And Kimberley knew that she would never be able to disillusion her mother about her true relationship with Harrison.

Her mother clipped a pearl hatpin in place. 'You're not having a honeymoon, then?'

'No.' Thank God. 'I'm feeding Georgia, and . . .' There was no reason to have a honeymoon in a marriage where there was no love involved.

'No matter,' said Mrs Ryan briskly. 'You're fortunate enough to be going back to a beautiful home—a lot of couples don't have that. There'll be time for honeymoons later. I just wish that your father was alive to see you.' She dabbed briefly at her eyes with a lace handkerchief, then pulled her shoulders back in a no-nonsense gesture. 'Come along, now, Kimberley—you don't want to be late for your own wedding!'

And in an attempt to cheer her mother up, and convince her that all was well, Kimberley was able to joke, 'But brides are *supposed* to be late for their own weddings, Mum!'

They walked the short distance to the church, and Kimberley was still smiling at something her mother had said to her when she walked into a church filled to bursting with flowers and saw Harrison waiting for her at the altar. Her heart turned over with love. He had chosen Duncan for his best man, and an intense and narrow-eyed look had come into his face when he'd asked her whether she minded that.

'I don't,' she'd answered. 'But Duncan might.'

But Duncan had not minded. In fact, he had been delighted, and so had Caroline, now his wife.

The buzz of conversation from the small congregation died down as Kimberley appeared in the nave of the church, and Harrison immediately turned round, his face impossibly grave and handsome, the suit he wore emphasising his height, the powerful breadth of shoulder, the long, elegant thrust of his legs. Sitting in the front pew to his right, his mother cradled Georgia, who was decked out for the day in an impossibly frilly white baby dress, bought especially from Harrods for the occasion by her father.

It was moving enough to have her mother give her away, but by the time Kimberley reached the altar and looked up into the serious grey eyes, then down again at Georgia's tiny head, her black hair almost hidden by the matching frilly bonnet, Kimberley was so choked up with emotion that she was unable to speak.

That was when Harrison took her hand and squeezed it, but this only made things worse, until he took a pristine white handkerchief from his top pocket and wiped at the tear which sparkled on her cheek, bending his head to whisper to her.

'You look very, very beautiful.'

And he said it in such a way that the words carried Kimberley through the ceremony. They came outside to a multi-coloured flurry of confetti and she heard some of the comments from some of the villagers who had come to stand at the back of the church to see the bride and groom.

'Why was she crying?'

'Hormones,' came the reply. 'She's only just had the baby.'

'Catch *me* crying, if I was marrying *him*!'

Some of the tension lifted now that the ceremony was over. Kimberley couldn't help it—she giggled, and Harrison looked down at her approvingly.

'That's better! Feel ready to face the reception?'

Not really. She would have preferred to have crept away, with him and Georgia. But perhaps it was better that they *were* going to the reception, since she was feeling very soppy and very vulnerable, and in that state there was no saying what she might do if she was actually left alone with Harrison. Her husband.

So they dutifully ate the magnificent feast of prawns and salmon and strawberries, all washed down with the finest vintage champagne, which Mrs Nash Senior had provided, and served in a marquee in the grounds of Brockbank House.

But, sitting next to Harrison, the baby nestled in the crook of his arm, Kimberley felt on a strange high, and it was nothing to do with the one and a half glasses of champagne she'd drunk. Something had happened to her there in the church, when he had wiped the tear away from her face. She had thought... thought... Thought what? That some deep spark of something approaching affection had flown from his eyes as he had stared down into hers? Or was she simply imagining that the gesture had been redolent of tenderness?

But his voice remained gentle when, after the speeches, he looked down at her with a smile. 'Want to go home now?' he asked.

Home. Her heart was going crazy as she met that soft grey stare. She nodded, her breath catching in her throat. 'I'd better go and get changed first.'

'Don't.' There was the glitter of sexual promise in his eyes as they skimmed over the way the cream silk clung to her full breasts like a second skin. 'I like it.'

Kimberley blushed like an eighteen-year-old. Crazy, *crazy* to let a silly little compliment affect her in this way. 'Thank you,' she said breathlessly. And then, because it seemed the safest thing to say, 'Georgia has been a poppet, hasn't she?'

He nodded. 'Personally, I think she's the best baby in the world, but—like you—I'm rather biased. Come on, let's say our goodbyes. Then I'll put her into the car.'

Fifteen minutes later they were speeding away, Georgia sound asleep in her baby-seat at the back. Harrison sat at the wheel of the large Bentley, Kimberley at his side.

He shot her a look. 'There. That wasn't too bad, was it?'

'No.' She stole a glance at him. 'Thanks.'

'For what?'

'For rescuing me in the church.'

His teeth gleamed white as he smiled. 'I've always liked rescuing maidens in distress.'

'Not much of a maiden,' she said wryly.

'No.' There was a pause. Then he said, in a kind of bitter voice, 'But you were, weren't you?'

Kimberley thought that she must have misheard him. '*What*?' she whispered incredulously.

'I was the first, wasn't I? Your first lover?'

'You mean you knew—all along?'

'Not all along.' She saw the hard mouth twist. 'No. Let's just say that it quickly became evident——'

'Harrison—you don't have to——'

'Oh, but I *do*,' he said bitterly. 'Why the hell didn't you tell me?'

She raised her brows. 'Do you think it would have made any difference?'

He gave her a quick, hard look. 'I'm not in the habit of seducing virgins,' he said. 'But I'd have been a damn sight more careful about contraception if I'd known.'

This hurt badly. It was as good as saying that they would not be here now if he had taken that simple precaution and hadn't she lulled herself, during the reception, into believing otherwise? Fool. Kimberley shut her eyes briefly, before opening them again. Don't get hurt, she willed herself. Or upset. Don't destroy what has been the most honest talk we've ever had with each other.

'But that night, even after you'd found out that I was a virgin, you still assumed that I was protected?' she probed. 'At least, that's what you said at the time.'

His hands tightened on the steering-wheel. 'I assumed that you would have told me if you weren't. Or, at least, that if you found yourself pregnant, you would have contacted me. When you didn't, I naturally took it for granted that we'd been——'

'Lucky?' she put in bitterly, before he could damn her with the word himself.

'I just wish you'd been a little more honest with me at the time.'

'I didn't think it was honesty that you were searching for that evening,' she told him candidly. 'You've always tended to make a lot of assumptions about me, haven't you, Harrison? For example, would you have really believed that I was a virgin if I'd told you?' she asked softly, and heard his long sigh.

'Probably not.'

She shrugged. That, too, hurt. It made her feel like some rapacious little tramp. 'Well, then, there's nothing more to be said, is there?'

'I rather think that there is,' he said quietly. 'I owe you an apology, for one thing.'

She forced a little laugh—it was the kind of brittle laugh she had heard other women use and she found it surprisingly easy to master. 'Forget it. Perhaps I should be flattered that you considered me so sexually experienced that it didn't occur to you that I might be otherwise.'

'As I think I told you once before—you seem to bring out the worst in me.'

'Oh, well, that's the way of the world,' she answered lightly. 'And, as I once told *you*—the feeling's entirely mutual.'

'I'm sorry,' he said simply.

She heard the self-recrimination in his voice, but she was honest enough to know that there had been no coercion on his part and she could not let him carry all the blame.

'Don't be. I love Georgia to bits.'

'And so do I.' His voice was very soft. 'And thank you, Kimberley.'

She paused in the act of removing her hat. 'What for?'

'For having her.'

She frowned. 'Meaning?'

'That there was always an alternative—which most people would perhaps have considered the more sensible option, given the circumstances.'

'Then it's a good thing I'm not most people,' she answered, but it was an effort to keep her voice steady, because that one very important compliment had gone a long way towards banishing some of the anger she felt towards him.

She saw him glance over at her again. 'What did you do with the cheque I gave you?' he asked suddenly.

Kimberley was astounded by his question, and apprehensive about his reasons for asking it. 'I cashed it,' she said.

'Yes, I know that—but what did you do with the money?'

'Why?'

He shrugged. 'Curiosity.'

'I spent it on expensive holidays and clothes,' she lied wildly.

'The truth!' he bit out tersely.

And now Kimberley was curious, too. 'And how do you know it isn't the truth?'

'Let's just call it a gut feeling.'

Kimberley sighed. 'I gave it away—to charity.'

'All of it?'

'Every penny!'

He nodded his head very slowly, as if he'd just worked out the answer to some ongoing and irksome problem. 'I should have guessed.'

'And why should you have?' whispered Kimberley, feeling that she, too, was on the brink of some tremendous discovery.

He shrugged. 'You have a particularly stubborn kind of pride, Kimberley—one which does not go hand in hand with accepting bribes.' Then he frowned. 'But why did you take it in the first place?'

To get him off her back, of course. But if she told him that he might draw his own conclusions as to why. Her mind cast around for a convincing alternative. 'Because I was angry with you—insulted that you thought you could buy me off. I thought I'd make you suffer—financially, at least. So I took your money from you and gave it away.'

Those intelligent grey eyes were too damned perceptive, she thought as she pretended to fiddle with the catch of her cream clutch-bag.

'But if you were simply angry with me then the most effective thing you could have done would have been to go ahead and marry Duncan.'

'But I couldn't marry Duncan. Not once I discovered that I was so...' She chose her next words carefully. 'Sexually attracted to you.'

He said nothing in reply, but she saw him give another small nod as he drove on, quite fast but very carefully. There was a more companionable silence between them as the powerful car ate up the miles, and she was aware that a truce, of sorts, had been unspokenly declared.

Kimberley felt an excitement growing within her. Didn't that conversation symbolise some kind of hope? His honestly spoken apology had warmed her—and his recognition that going ahead and having the baby on her own had not been the easiest option. And he had, it seemed, credited her with the integrity of not accepting his cheque simply for financial gain.

On such a basis was there not room for respect and liking to grow? And these, hand in hand with the dynamite of their sexual chemistry, wouldn't these be enough to become the foundations of a satisfactory marriage—if not the love-locked union her heart yearned for?

Should she allow their wedding-day to draw to its natural conclusion? Should she allow him to make love to her tonight? Kimberley gave a little shiver of excitement. Could she honestly say no to him?

It was almost seven when they arrived back in Kew, but as they drew up outside the large, imposing house all her old insecurities about him came flooding back. Kimberley felt a sudden sense of shyness as Harrison switched the engine off, wondering where they went from here, afraid to look him in the eye in case she discovered that the qualities she had attributed to him in the car had all turned out to be figments of her imagination. She was therefore ridiculously pleased when Georgia gave a little squawk of protest.

'She must be hungry,' she said hastily, and leapt out of the car to open up the back door. 'I'd better feed her.'

He followed her, and when she turned and saw the grim set of his face her heart sank, but she felt a certain sense of relief too. She thanked her lucky stars that she hadn't allowed a false sense of security to lull her into doing something foolish, like letting him know how she felt about him. And, if she was being brutally honest, if she allowed their relationship to become properly intimate would she really be able to stop herself from telling him?

She remembered how she'd been that night of the party—she'd had to force herself not to smother him with soft and soppy words—and that had been just *one* night. Imagine every night. In his arms. The act of love. She'd be bound to slip up and tell him she loved him, and where would that lead her? A declared one-sided relationship would surely be doomed? She knew what happened to unrequited love; everyone did. The ones who loved lost all their self-respect, and the objects of their love eventually despised them for their devotion.

Waiting for them in the hall, her hands primly clasped in front of her waist, stood Sarah—her blonde hair gleaming, her brown and white uniform crisply pressed as she held her arms out for Georgia.

'Congratulations,' she said in her rather colourless voice, her eyes, as always, fixed steadily on Harrison.

'Thank you, Sarah,' he said, his deep voice warming in a smile, and Kimberley felt an acute stab of jealousy as Sarah gazed back at him.

'Mrs Caithness has laid out a cold dinner for two in the small dining-room, as you ordered, sir.'

Which was what a real honeymoon couple might have done, thought Kimberley—eaten a meal together and gone upstairs to make love.

But the difference was that this was all farce. And if she hadn't been so certain that she couldn't play-act indifference towards him—especially not to-night, after the heightened emotion of the marriage ceremony—then maybe she might have gone through with it.

But, being forced to hide her feelings from him, she would simply have felt like a lamb being fattened up for the sacrifice.

She found herself staring into a pair of quizzical grey eyes. 'Well, Kimberley?'

A simple enough question, but she knew that it had many shades of meaning. He was asking her yes or no, and her answer had nothing to do with the meal he'd had prepared.

'I'm not hungry,' she answered coolly. 'And I must see to the baby.' And, so saying, she took Georgia from Sarah's arms and mounted the stairs towards the nursery, unable to miss the hostile fire which flamed in the depths of those smoky grey eyes or, indeed, the smug little smirk of triumph which Sarah flashed in Harrison's direction.

'But what shall I do with all the food?' she heard Sarah asking plaintively.

'Do what you want with it.' She heard his indifferent reply. 'I'm going out!'

And the last thing she heard was the front door closing behind him.

CHAPTER TEN

KIMBERLEY had realised the mistake she had made within hours.

The day following the wedding she stumbled blearily down to breakfast, Georgia having woken several times during the night, but even if she hadn't done it wouldn't have made any difference, since Kimberley hadn't been able to sleep. She'd spent a miserable night in her old room, lying awake and listening for the sound of Harrison returning home. But he hadn't returned home.

Just after midnight she had crept downstairs, thinking that perhaps he might have come in and fallen asleep in the drawing-room, but there had been no sign of him. Even though she'd eaten nothing since the reception she had felt too sick at heart for food, but she had been very thirsty, and something had made her look into the dining-room to see whether Sarah had removed the food. She had.

Kimberley had felt tears prickle the back of her eyes as she'd seen the beautiful spray of white roses, stephanotis and freesia in the centre of the table— it looked so very bridal. Had Harrison chosen that? she wondered. Kimberley had sighed, thinking what a mess everything was.

She had just been turning to go when she'd seen a slim silver-wrapped package lying at one of the two places, and, her curiosity alerted, she had moved closer and seen that the small card attached to it bore her name.

She had hesitated for only a moment, then, with trembling fingers, she had torn the paper off. Inside had been a navy leather box stamped with the name of one of London's most exclusive jewellers. She had flipped the top off, and there—dazzlingly bright against the black velvet of the interior—had been a necklace of diamonds and aquamarines—starry and spectacular and utterly beautiful.

Kimberley had closed the box and held it over her heart. Why had he bought her such a gift? So costly and so exquisite. As a peace-offering? She'd closed her eyes, knowing that she had spoiled it all, and, after fetching herself a glass of milk from the kitchen, had crept miserably back upstairs to her room, the box still clutched in her hand, to lie awake, still listening for him.

And, apart from Georgia waking for her feeds, the night had been one of long silence.

This morning Harrison was sitting at the table in the dining-room, drinking coffee and eating eggs and reading the financial pages of the newspaper. He barely looked up when she entered the room.

'Good morning,' said Kimberley.

He barely glanced at her. The grey eyes were cold as a winter's sea. 'Is it?' he mocked.

Kimberley tried very hard to behave normally. She fetched herself some scrambled eggs from the silver tureen on the side, added a few mushrooms and a slice of toast, sat down and poured herself some coffee. Then she smiled at him, but met no answering response. His features might have been hewn from granite, they were so uncaring and so unresponsive.

She drew a deep breath. 'I—saw the necklace you left for me. It's very beautiful,' she said.

'Forget it,' he said dismissively.

'No, really——'

'If you'd prefer some other stones, then you can always exchange it,' he said. 'Or sell it,' he added insultingly.

Kimberley almost gasped aloud at the venom in his voice. He'd been cold with her in the past but never this cold. She had turned down his intimate supper last night, and his gift. Had he, then, she wondered with a sickening lurch of her heart, gone out to find solace in the arms of someone else? Clamping down the murderous jealousy which flooded hotly through her veins, she clenched her trembling hands on her lap beneath the heavy damask of the white tablecloth, where he could not see them. She had to know. She *had* to know.

She narrowed her blue eyes at him. 'You didn't come in last night,' she said, in a voice which was remarkable for its steadiness.

'That's right,' he drawled.

'May I ask where you went?'

'You may not.'

'Did you—did you sleep with somebody else?' she blurted out, then cringed at the total lack of pride inherent in her question.

'Why,' he drawled mockingly, 'should that concern you? You don't want me, do you,

Kimberley? Or rather, you *do*—you're just not honest enough to admit it. Perhaps you like playing games; maybe it turns you on to dangle your sexual favours. But I'm not into games, and I'm not your plaything. Fight the attraction all you like—but don't for one moment imagine that you're going to condemn me to a life of celibacy.'

His brutal frankness took her breath away. She stared at that cold, handsome face, at the icy chips of his hard, cruel eyes, and at that moment she really and truly hated him, with a strength of feeling which left her speechless but which showed in the frosty glitter of her blue eyes.

'You—*brute*,' she accused him in a hollow whisper. 'You absolute brute.'

He actually laughed. 'What's that—cue for the brute to demonstrate his brutishness by pulling the fastidious Kimberley into his arms and taking her by force? That would solve your problem for you, wouldn't it, my dear, and salve your conscience? You could have all the pleasure without having been weak enough yourself to actually *admit* that you wanted it. Well, sorry, sweetheart—but I'm not taking the bait.' He pushed his chair back and rose from the table.

'I'm going away for a week on business,' he said harshly. 'And while I'm away you might like to consider when you want to go back to work. I don't imagine, given the current state of affairs between us, that you want to hang around the house any more than you have to.'

She stared at him incredulously. 'You mean you're happy for us to live like *this*—constantly bickering and squabbling?'

His hard, cynical mouth twisted. 'Happy? Hardly the word I would use. No, Kimberley, I'm not happy. But you're the one who has chosen to live like this. Remember that. And don't try leaving while I'm away. At least, not with Georgia. I told you—I want my daughter, and I'll do anything to keep her.'

Kimberley swallowed. 'Very well,' she said steadily. 'I'll be here when you get back.' And she couldn't damp down the desire to try and hurt him as much as he had hurt her. 'And, as you seem to have acquired yourself a bed-partner, I'll have to start looking around myself.'

His eyes darkened. 'Not in this house, you won't,' he threatened.

'No. I won't do that. I'll just stay out all night, as you did.'

A muscle worked angrily in the side of his face. 'And I suppose that dear James is to be the lucky recipient of your desires, is he?' he ground out.

And two could play at this game, Kimberley decided. 'That really has nothing to do with you,' she answered coolly.

He stared at her for a long minute, passion and fire and fury making the grey eyes smoulder, and she thought that he *was* about to stride across the room and start making angry love to her. Then he abruptly made a curse and turned his back on her.

But at the door he paused, and when he turned around again his face was perfectly composed.

'Oh, I meant to tell you. The evening after I arrive back, I've decided to hold a party here. It'll give some of my friends a chance to meet you, since you refused to allow any of them to come to the wedding. They've been asking me why I'm keeping you hidden away.' His mouth twisted. 'If they only knew.'

She lifted her head proudly. 'And presumably they don't?'

'No. And I'd like to keep it that way.' He paused. 'I want you to be my hostess.'

He made it sound like a whore, but she bit back her angry reply. She was going to have to come up with some kind of solution to what was promising to be an intolerable living situation, and much more anger and recrimination between them was not going to solve anything.

And all this bitterness seemed to stem from her refusal to dine with him last night.

Why?

It couldn't just be the physical thing. It just couldn't. A man like Harrison could have just about any woman he wanted. And he had done, she thought, with angry desperation. Last night. And he would go on doing so, just as long as she held him at arm's length.

If only she had the strength to leave here, to see if he really would fight her in the courts for Georgia's custody. Surely as a mother she held most of the cards?

But she didn't have the strength, and she wasn't at all sure that the reason had anything to do with the costs or publicity incurred by a court case.

He was regarding her quizzically. 'So you'll be at the party?' he enquired softly.

'Yes, Harrison,' she echoed on a sigh. 'I'll be at the party.'

CHAPTER ELEVEN

IT WAS a Friday afternoon, exactly seven days later, and Kimberley was sitting in the magnificent yellow drawing-room, which overlooked the beautiful gardens at the back of the house, when she heard the front door slam shut.

'Hello?' came the deep sound of Harrison's voice.

She took a huge, huge breath. She had had a lot of time on her hands for thinking during those seven days—she had decided what her strategy was going to be, and she was going to stick to it. The time for conciliation was long overdue.

'I'm in here,' she called.

She heard his footsteps moving towards her, and then the door opened and he stood there looking down at her, where she was curled up on the tartan sofa, a magazine by her side, Georgia at her feet, asleep in her tiny chair.

She stared back at him, trying not to feast her eyes on him. As always, just the sight of him did strange things to her heartrate; it was as though he electrified the whole atmosphere of a room just by being in it.

He'd left in a suit, but now he wore jeans. The jeans were very old and faded, and fitted so snugly to his buttocks and thighs that they might have been sprayed on. A white T-shirt was tucked into the jeans, and it clung lovingly to the muscles which rippled in his upper chest and arms. His hair was ruffled and he needed a shave. He looked, she realised, much younger than his thirty-three years— and unbelievably sexy.

The week he'd been gone had seemed like an eternity. She had missed him like hell, although she had wondered how it was possible to miss someone you fought with the whole time.

She, too, was wearing jeans—black jeans with a black T-shirt—and her thick black hair cascaded freely down her back. She hadn't been expecting him back this early, and had planned to change into something a little smarter, but now she was glad she hadn't done. She would have felt a fool. She saw his eyes flicker to the swell of her breasts, felt them tingle into life.

On the other hand, she thought, this T-shirt was awfully clingy, and maybe that hadn't been such a good idea either. Kimberley crossed her arms over her chest protectively, and she saw the sardonic curve of his mouth.

His eyes softened as he looked down at his daughter, fast asleep and sucking her thumb in her little baby-chair. 'She's grown,' he observed, shaking his head a little. 'Incredible. Only a week, and she's changed.'

Her heart turned over at the tenderness written on his face, and she nodded. 'Yes. She's put on weight,' she said proudly, wondering whether this was the shape of things to come. Polite little platitudes about their daughter—just about their only neutral ground, really.

He was frowning. 'Something's different.'

She waited.

'She doesn't usually sleep down here.'

'No, that's right.' Because Sarah had insisted that she always take her nap in her nursery.

He looked around the room. The bright pink teddy he'd sent from France was sitting on the sofa next to an orange rabbit his brother and Caroline had bought for the baby. They clashed like crazy, but Kimberley was certain that Georgia loved them. People said that babies didn't recognise things until they were six weeks old, but she didn't believe them—not babies as intelligent as Georgia, anyway!

Harrison smiled when he saw the teddy. 'And there are more of her toys down here than usual.'

Another of Sarah's edicts. Kimberley could just hear her prim little voice. 'We don't want the house looking like a kindergarten, do we? Not for Mr Nash coming home!'

'Where's Sarah?' he asked, suddenly and perceptively.

She could justify exactly what she'd done, but her heart beat faster all the same. 'I've fired her,' she said calmly.

He looked at her as though he'd misheard. 'You've done *what*?' he demanded.

'I've fired her.'

'Would you mind telling me why?'

'Sure. I didn't agree with her way of bringing up babies.'

He raised his eyebrows. 'And you're the expert, I suppose?' he enquired sarcastically. 'On babies?'

'Yes, I am, actually, Harrison—with this particular baby, certainly. Besides, I've been reading books on the subject all week. Four of them, actually.'

He was staring at her in bemusement. 'Four books and she knows more than a girl who spent two years training?'

'Yes!' she snapped, conciliation forgotten for the moment. 'I *want* to demand-feed, and I *do* want to pick her up when she cries. And what I *don't* want is to hide away all signs that she exists. She happens to live here, too—and I don't believe that babies shouldn't be seen and shouldn't be heard! But, more than that—and I'm sorry if this offends you Harrison—I didn't happen to like Sarah. I thought she was prim and smug and narrow-minded, and not particularly intelligent. And if you think that I'm going to let someone like that bring my daughter up, well—I'm not, basically.' She paused for breath, wondering how he'd take it.

'Wow,' he said softly. 'That's some speech!'

'And I mean every word of it.'

'I can see that.'

'And you don't mind?'

He shrugged the broad shoulders. 'It isn't me it will affect, is it? It's you. So, tell me, are you planning to replace Sarah with someone who isn't prim and smug and narrow-minded? Or had you intended to take her into the office with you?'

And now it was time for her next bombshell. 'I'm not going back to the office.'

'*What*?' he asked in disbelief.

'I'm taking some time off—to bring Georgia up.'

'But your career is very important to you,' he pointed out.

'So is she,' she said quietly.

'And what are you going to do all day? Bake bread?'

She found herself giggling, still high with the excitement and amazement of it all—of discovering that this was what she really *wanted* to do. 'I might,' she said. 'As well as making play-dough. There will also be long walks and finger-painting——'

He held his hand up, but there was a glint of amusement lighting his eyes. 'Enough! I get the idea. And if it's what you want——'

'It is.' She saw him frown. 'If it bothers you that I won't be earning——'

The beautiful grey eyes narrowed, and the amused glint became a distant memory. 'I don't give a damn about that,' he said roughly.

And then, perhaps because they had exhausted the subject of Georgia, he moved away, his shoulders tense. 'You haven't forgotten the party, have you?'

In truth, she'd scarcely given it a thought. 'No, of course not,' she said stiffly.

'I've organised for our guests to arrive at seven-thirty for eight tomorrow evening. The caterers will be here most of the afternoon. Does that suit you?'

Kimberley swallowed. She hated that formal tone he could adopt, as though she were someone he'd just met at a cocktail party and not the mother of his child. 'Perfectly,' she answered coolly. 'Can you give me a rough idea of numbers?'

'There will be about fifty,' he said curtly. 'But you won't need to do anything. I've had my secretary send out invitations—she's arranged everything through the office.'

'How nice,' said Kimberley nastily. 'I'm surprised that you didn't ask *her* to be your hostess for you.'

'I damn well wish that I had done!' he ground out, then, with an effort, he seemed to gain some ascendancy over his temper, so that when he spoke again it was very slowly—as though he were explaining something to a simpleton. 'I thought that you'd be too tired, and too tied up with the baby to want to go to the trouble of organising a party.'

It was as though he'd retreated from her, thought Kimberley. She might have been some servant or some underling from the way in which he addressed her.

'And is it to be formal?' she asked.

'Black tie,' he told her. 'And now, if you'll excuse me, I must go and change.'

'Will you——?' She forced herself to ask it. 'Will you be in for dinner tonight?'

He shook his head. 'I'm eating out. I thought that you'd probably prefer it.' And he left the room without another word.

Kimberley watched him leave, her neck and back held stiff and proud, determined that he shouldn't find out that she had asked Mrs Caithness to leave them something easy for supper—something which she could heat up herself. She had planned, or rather hoped, for a companionable meal together.

But it seemed that she was being given no chance to achieve that.

The following evening she was as nervous as a schoolgirl going to her first ever party as she got ready. Would his friends, naturally curious to meet her, see that he was unhappy? And would they understandably blame her for that unhappiness?

After she'd fed Georgia, bathed and changed her and settled her down in her cot for the night, Kimberley turned her attention to her appearance.

She spent ages deciding what to wear, eventually choosing the most dramatic outfit in her wardrobe. To hell with it! She'd had it made up on a business trip to Hong Kong, and had never seen anything like it in England. The tiny chemise top and long, flowing skirt were in vibrant turquoise silk—material as soft as a sigh, which fluttered against her breasts and long legs. The matching matador jacket and wide cummerbund were in a patterned silk brocade in the same turquoise teamed with jade-green and swirls of kingfisher-blue.

Her hair was fixed into a dramatic topknot, kept in place with two silver combs studded with tiny turquoise chips. She did her make-up dramatically too—with kohl pencil outlining her almond-shaped ice-blue eyes and a bold sweep of a deeper blue eyeshadow emphasising their unusual pale colour. Even her lips looked fuller than usual after she'd carefully painted them with coral gloss.

She stepped back from the mirror, satisfied with her appearance, but slightly in awe of the sophisticated image which stared back at her. But at least

from the look of her no one would have any idea
that inside she was as nervous as hell about meeting
Harrison's friends.

She had had nothing to do with the prepara-
tions; Harrison and his secretary had seen to all
that. And how! There were people to serve the
drinks and people to take the guests' coats. The
food would be cooked and served by professional
caterers. They had even arranged for a florist to
arrange blooms in every one of the five reception
rooms.

'And what do you want me to do?' Kimberley
had asked him over lunch.

'Just be there,' he'd said briefly, but his face had
been so cold that she'd wondered if he wanted her
there at all.

But when she came down the staircase, to find
him waiting for her in the entrance hall, his eyes
narrowed as he took in her appearance, and something in the humourless upward tilt of his mouth
made her wonder if she was completely overdressed.

'Is this OK?' she asked.

'Perfectly OK,' he answered, his voice becoming
less of a whisper, more of a threat. 'That is if you
don't mind every man in the room wondering
whether the body underneath all that silk could
possibly be as exquisite as it promises. But perhaps
that was your intention—to have every hot-blooded
male under the age of ninety lusting after you.'

'You're hateful,' she mumbled, and was half inclined to run back upstairs and seek refuge in her
little black dress when there was a loud peal on
the doorbell.

'Smile, Kimberley,' he ordered softly. 'And let's play newly-weds.'

Soon all the staff hired for the evening were hard at work, and within half an hour all the guests had arrived and were being served with champagne and canapés in the drawing-room.

Although it was early September, the weather had been so glorious that the newspapers were calling it another Indian summer, and the large French windows at the back of the house had been opened on to the garden.

Harrison introduced her to a stream of people, including his secretary, Anne Lyons—and Kimberley despised herself for the relief which flooded over her when she discovered that not only was Anne a Mrs but a grandmother too! There were men Harrison had been to boarding-school with, and others he'd known at various stages of his climb up the corporate ladder. There were people from the States, and from Europe, too. Most of them with partners.

And there were women on their own, as well. Women who smilingly took Kimberley's hand and congratulated her—some more genuinely than others. Including a strikingly statuesque young model in her early twenties called Tania who Kimberley recognised immediately—she'd broken all records for the number of magazine covers her face had graced that year. Close up, the girl was even more stunning than she appeared in photographs, with waist-length hair the colour of a glossy brown conker and the most amazing long-lashed violet eyes.

Kimberley could sense the model's antagonism towards her immediately, although it was reasonably well-hidden by the huge flashing smile with its perfect teeth. But as the evening wore on Kimberley could see something in the way the younger woman monopolised Harrison—or maybe it was him monopolising her.

And suddenly she knew.

The glass of champagne she had raised to her lips remained untasted as realisation, stark and brutal, made itself clear to her. She knew by the way Tania darted him her saucy smile, and by the way he jokingly pretended to pull her hair, bending his head to listen to something she said. Something in their body language spoke volumes, and she knew with a blinding instinct which ripped at her heart like a newly sharpened sword that there had been intimacy between them.

Had been?

Her world blurred out of focus as she realised that the past tense might be inappropriate.

That night he'd stayed out—had he stayed with Tania? This week he'd been away—had his 'business' been spurious? Kimberley closed her eyes and almost swayed, terribly afraid that she might do something really stupid, like faint.

And then, delicate as some beautiful wraith, Tania suddenly appeared by her side, looking down at the full glass of champagne which Kimberley was clutching like a lifeline.

The violet eyes glittered like costly amethysts. 'Hey, you've been nursing that glass all evening! Not in the party mood?'

Kimberley shook her head. 'I'm a little tired,' she answered, trying not to sound as though her world was threatening to crumble around her.

As if of one accord, they both looked to where Harrison stood, saying something to a group of people, effortlessly dominating not just the group who were listening to him with rapt attention but the entire party. He stood out among every other man there—and what woman wouldn't want him? thought Kimberley with a sinking heart.

'He's mine, you know,' came the softly spoken threat beside her, and Kimberley stared at Tania in amazement, certain that she had misheard what the model had said.

'I'm sorry?'

'No, you heard right,' said Tania nonchalantly. 'I was just warning you off.'

'But I'm married to him,' said Kimberley quietly. 'Remember?'

'Are you?' the girl challenged, her bottom lip pouting in a way that should have looked truculent but instead managed to look very, very provocative. 'You don't act like you're married. Harrison's so uptight, he looks as though he might snap—and you've hardly talked to him all night.'

'I'm married to him,' said Kimberley again, her voice dignified. But her hands were shaking.

The beautiful violet eyes were suddenly made ugly by the expression in them. 'Yeah, you're married to him. Know why? Because of the baby. And because possession is nine-tenths of the law, and a father who has never even lived with his daughter doesn't have much say. Harrison figures that pretty

soon your life will be so miserable you'll be glad
to walk away—and this way he'll have clout in
court, when it comes to custody.' She smiled. 'Then
he'll come running to me,' she finished on a soft
threat.

Kimberley managed somehow not to flinch, then,
very deliberately, she turned her back on the model
and walked to the end of the garden, a smile fixed
to her face, afraid to stop moving in case she broke
down and made the most appalling scene.

She found herself the seclusion of the rose-bower,
hiding in its sweetly scented shade, letting her cheek
rub against the velvety petals of a late pink bloom
while she willed her thundering heart to slow down
and the dizzy, sick feeling at the pit of her stomach
to go away, so that she could put her troubled
thoughts into some kind of order.

From here she could watch, unobserved, as Tania
picked her way across the lawn and joined
Harrison's group, immediately convulsing into a fit
of giggles at something he was saying. And
Kimberley knew that she could no longer carry on
ignoring the situation she was in.

Things between them were fast becoming unbearable. Harrison had laid the rules down at the
very beginning. A marriage without its physical side
meant that he would look elsewhere. And could she
bear that?

Never.

She loved him; indeed, she had always loved him.
There had never been anyone else, and she knew
herself well enough to know that there never
would be.

He, on the other hand, seemed to despise her when he wasn't lusting after her body.

But...

Again her mind flew back to the day of the wedding—his gentleness towards her in the church, the conversation in the car, which had cleared the air, paved the way for a tentative truce. And perhaps, if it hadn't been for her highly emotional state and the sight of Sarah standing waiting for them, she might have done the most sensible thing and had supper with him and gone to bed with him—and they could have started off the marriage so differently.

It was not what she wanted; the question was whether it would be enough.

She stared through the gathering darkness at the tall and lithe form of him, head and shoulders above all the other men—and in more ways than just stature. She remembered the way he'd stayed with her during labour, his compassion in refusing to let her face that on her own. And he had done that knowing that she had kept his child a secret from him.

The question was—did she have the courage to show him that she wanted him, that she was prepared to change?

And then she saw Tania affectedly sweeping her hair back off her brow—her tiny black velvet mini-dress barely skimming her pert little bottom—and Kimberley's heart hardened.

Harrison was *her* man, and she knew how much he wanted her. She knew that in his arms she had a strange kind of power over him—as much as he had over her.

And tonight she had the perfect opportunity to show him, to show his friends—to show scheming little wannabes like Tania—that Harrison was spoken for.

She drank the glass of champagne quickly, and as the rush of the dry cold bubbles went fizzing throughout her bloodstream she strolled back through the garden.

She knew that people watched her—it was perfectly normal that they should watch the hostess, the woman who had married their friend—and she knew the precise moment when Harrison's grey eyes joined theirs, knew by the prickle of the tiny hairs at the back of her long neck and the shiver of anticipation which crept up her spine. Very deliberately she stared back at him, then raised her empty glass in toast.

Unselfconsciously, heady with the excitement of what she was planning to do, she stood alone, proud and beautiful as a statue, allowing her glass to be filled with mineral water and sipping it. And her eyes never left Harrison's handsome and mobile face.

She knew that he carried on speaking but that his thoughts were elsewhere—on her. She must only have stood there on her own for seconds, and yet time and time again she was aware of his eyes raking over her, questioning, probing.

In a couple of minutes two men and their wives joined her, complimenting her on the party, and she was chatting easily to them when, out of the corner of her eye, she saw Harrison move away from his group and come over to join them.

'Hello, darling,' she murmured.

It was a term of affection she had never used before, exactly the kind of thing which a newly married woman might say to her husband, and yet, not surprisingly, he frowned, and she saw the light of challenge fire in the back of the magnificent grey eyes.

She met the challenge full-on, her blue eyes widening with an unmistakable message, and she heard the soft inrush of his breath, felt the immediate flowering of her body as she saw his eyes darken with the same message he must have read in hers.

She wanted to leave the group and she wanted to take her jacket off, since tiny beads of sweat had formed on her forehead, but she didn't dare. She knew that her nipples were as erect and as excited as if he were actually caressing them, but she remembered, too, his earlier words, about her outfit enticing others. She didn't want him to think that. This was for him—all for him. No one else.

She didn't say anything; she didn't have to. Every fibre of her being spoke the message for her. She didn't know for how long they stood there, just that the need to have him touch her had grown so overpowering that she knew she would have to do something soon, or die.

She saw the tense lines of his face, the corded bunching of the muscles at his neck, and knew that he felt it too. She put her arm through his and rested her head against his shoulder. 'Can I talk to you for a moment?' she murmured, so that only he could hear, but the sultry tone of invitation was evident.

He tensed. Seemed to hesitate. But only for a moment. 'Please excuse us,' he said smoothly to the two couples, who were tactfully carrying on their conversation, seemingly unaware of the sexual currents which were fizzing and sizzling between the two of them.

As soon as they were out of earshot he dipped his head to speak softly into her ear. 'Shall we go for a walk around the garden?'

'No,' she said, in a low voice.

'But you wanted to talk?'

'Not here,' she said urgently, desire threatening to overwhelm her while her courage threatened to flee. 'Inside!'

He heard the note of raw hunger which deepened her voice to a husky whisper, took one look at her tense, white face, her eyes looking huge and dark in contrast, and unlinked her arm, placed her hand very firmly in his, and took her towards the house.

She was unable to speak, but Harrison paused now and then to exchange a word with their guests. To an outside observer they might just have been doing the kind of thing which party-givers always had to do, no matter how much help they had—checking that everything was running smoothly—but Kimberley thought she saw Tania start when she observed the feral glitter in Harrison's eyes as he led her inside the house after what had been the longest walk of her entire life.

He led her straight into his study, then let her go and turned to face her, his face as non-committal as a judge's.

'Well, Kimberley?'

He wasn't, she realised, going to give her any help at all. She swallowed convulsively.

'You said that you wanted to speak to me,' he observed coolly.

He gave the impression of having little time, or patience, and Kimberley made up her mind. There was no way she could back out of this now.

Casually she strolled over to the door, locked it, and put the key on his desk.

He raised his eyebrows but still said nothing.

She thought of what some women might do in this situation—a slow and seductive striptease, which would send him out of his mind—but she scotched that idea immediately. Her heart was thundering so loudly in her chest and her hands trembling so much that she knew there was only one thing in the world she could do, and she went over to him, raised herself up on tiptoe, put her arms around his neck and kissed him.

There was an infinitesimal second when rejection seemed a very real possibility, when the hard, sculpted lines of his mouth remained passive beneath the soft caress of her lips. But it was no more than the briefest fragment of time, and he reached his arms out to encircle her slender waist, deepening the kiss so sweetly and so provocatively that Kimberley melted under the onslaught.

They explored each other's mouths as though it was the first time they had ever kissed—and in a way perhaps it was, thought Kimberley, through the hot mists of passion and desire. For in that kiss was a new understanding—born of mutual need, mutual honesty and, for Kimberley at least, commitment. And not just a commitment that she would end up in his bed that night, but much more than that—a commitment that she would give the marriage a real go. And who knew what would happen if they both did that?

His mouth never leaving hers, he slipped his hand beneath the turquoise silk of her chemise to find her unfettered breast, cupping it in his hand and smiling against her mouth as he felt her helpless sigh. Her heartrate accelerated as she felt desire pool, then escalate out of control, so that she was pulled helplessly along, caught up in its powerful current.

So it was like being doused with ice-water when he suddenly raised his head and stared down at her shocked, mutinous face, a regretful look in the grey eyes. 'Kimberley,' he said, mock-seriously, 'you are very, very beautiful, and I want you very, very much, but I'm afraid that we'd better postpone this until later, or I'm not going to be in a fit state to go back to our guests.'

For answer, she raised her mouth greedily to his, running her hands deliberately down the white silk of his dress shirt, feeling him move with impatient frustration as she brushed further down, over the flat hardness of his stomach, and even further, where he was harder still...

He tore his mouth away, his words clipped and indistinct, barely recognisable. 'Kimberley, you realise what's going to happen in a minute if you don't——?'

'Yes,' she murmured.

He ground the words out with an effort. 'I'm going to have to take you right now——'

Her breathing was laboured. 'But you're not taking, Harrison,' she managed softly. 'I'm giving.'

He gave a small groan as he cupped her buttocks and gathered her roughly against him, his hands pulling the dress up her long legs impatiently, until it was gathered in rucks over her hips, so that only the tiniest scrap of her satin and lace panties covered her.

Very deliberately he pushed her back against the wall, his fingers moving to find her flowering moistness, and she gave a startled little moan of pleasure.

He caught her mouth again, murmuring something that sounded sweet and indistinct, and she felt him unzipping himself. She whispered her pleasure into his mouth, with soft little cries. His urgency was evident, since he didn't even bother to remove her bikini pants, just impatiently moved the fabric aside and thrust into her with such power that she was sure that consciousness slipped away from her for a second.

She noticed that he had stilled, and she looked up at him, gazing with wonderment into his dazed grey eyes.

'Oh, God, Kimberley,' he said, in a voice which verged on desperation. 'You feel so good.'

'Do I?' Her eyes closed, to hide her longing for softer words than these.

'Mmm.' He moved inside her slowly and she felt colour scorch over her cheeks. 'So *tight*.'

'Do I really?'

'Mmm. You know you do.'

'I thought—— *Oh*!' She clung frantically to his shoulders as he thrust against her.

'What?' he murmured provocatively.

'That it would be different—after the baby.'

'It is,' he said softly, still with those great slow sweeps which filled her completely. 'It's even better. But then perhaps it's because it's been so long...'

And suddenly she wanted to shatter his control. She didn't want him to move with that perfect provocation, which showed his consummate skill as a lover. She moved her hips urgently against his, changing the speed.

His eyes flew open. 'Don't——' he warned.

'Don't, what?'

'Don't do——' But he never finished the sentence, for he caught her rhythm and transmuted it into something which defied all description, so that if he was no longer in control then neither was she. She felt the heat building and building, until it became exquisitely unbearable, and the universe shattered and Kimberley found herself sobbing as he lost himself in the same dark whirlpool of fulfilment, her name torn from his lips in a shout which didn't sound at all like Harrison's voice.

They stayed like that, locked in that intimate embrace for a minute or two, and she felt his shoulders shaking. She realised that he was laughing.

'What,' she demanded, 'is so funny?'

He lifted her chin up and stared down into her eyes, his mouth quirking with sensual humour. 'I've never been seduced by a woman before.'

'And did you like it?' she whispered, reaching up to kiss his neck to hide her face, afraid that the love-light shining from her eyes might blind him.

'What do you think?'

'Want to do it some more?' she murmured.

He gingerly pulled away from her. 'Later, you beautiful and tempting minx.' He looked her up and down as he adjusted his clothing and helped to smooth her skirt down into place.

'You look quite normal, considering...' he mused. 'Your cheeks are a little flushed, of course, and your eyes are very bright. You are, you know, Kimberley, a rather amazing woman.' And he lifted one of her hands to his lips and gently kissed it, and Kimberley felt overwhelmed with love.

'Oh, Harrison,' she said foolishly, breathlessly, her heart still thundering in her ears.

'We'd better get back to the party,' he said softly. 'We can talk later.'

'I really ought to go upstairs and shower,' she said wryly.

'No, don't.' He bent his head to plant a kiss on her mouth. 'Stay exactly as you are, so that every time I look at you I can remember what we've just been doing, and imagine what I'm going to do to you once everyone has gone.'

And he unlocked the door, took her by the hand and led her back to the party.

CHAPTER TWELVE

'SO WHAT brought all that on?' Harrison asked as
Kimberley came down the stairs. The silk of her
long skirt was still vaguely crumpled, and she wondered whether anyone had noticed.

All the guests had gone, all the party debris was
cleared away, and the staff had departed too.
Kimberley had gone up to check on Georgia, and
was about to join Harrison downstairs for a
nightcap. If the truth were known, she didn't really
want a nightcap—or rather, she didn't want to sit
down analysing her wild behaviour of earlier that
evening, when she'd taken him into his study and
seduced with the single-mindedness of a concubine.

She sat down opposite him and met his steady
grey stare reluctantly.

'And don't say "All what?", when you know
perfectly well that I'm referring to that extraordinary little scene of a couple of hours ago, which
is threatening to put my blood pressure up into
dangerous heights just by thinking about it.'

'Harrison, please,' she beseeched, but there was
no mercy in his speculative smile.

'Don't go all coy on me, Kimberley,' he murmured. 'I think I rather prefer you taking the in-
itiative.' He got up and poured out two small glasses
of calvados and handed her one. 'I repeat—what
brought it on?'

A new honesty, she had decided—or rather, as much honesty as their relationship could stand. She knew that the knowledge of her unrequited love would bring about the destruction of their already tenuous relationship in its wake, but there was no reason for him not to know about Tania.

'I spoke to Tania,' she told him, in a colourless voice. 'Or rather—she spoke to me.'

He sipped his drink. The grey eyes were as cool as a glacier. 'Oh?'

'Yes.' Her voice sounded bright. 'She told me— well, lots of things, really.'

'Care to let me in on a few of them?'

'Just that she wanted you. And that we didn't look married. And then I remembered what you said about me not condemning you to a life of celibacy, and I knew what I had to do.'

Some light died in his eyes, leaving them forbiddingly cold. 'You mean—seduce me? In order to stop Tania getting her hooks into me? That was very territorial of you, Kimberley.'

She turned towards him, exasperated now—and confused. 'Well, that was what you wanted, wasn't it?'

His mouth was unsmiling as he rose to his feet with seductive intent written all over his face and moved towards her. 'Yes,' he agreed, a new note to his voice—and she wasn't sure that she liked it very much at all. 'That's what I wanted.'

She stared up at him in bewilderment as he took the glass from her hand and put it down, then swept her up into his arms, as if he'd been auditioning for a remake of *Gone with the Wind* and carried her up the staircase and into her bedroom.

It was as though he was reasserting his authority and dominance after what had happened earlier—for if she had held the power in their earlier encounter then he certainly had it now, as he slowly but ruthlessly stripped the clothes from her body.

It seemed to be a deliberate demonstration of how he could bring her trembling to the brink, time and time again, until she was half weeping with desperation, and she opened her eyes to see him pulling the black bow-tie off with impatient disregard.

And while he undressed he still touched her, stroked her, every single inch of her, as he efficiently removed the rest of the clothes from his body, keeping her at such an incredible fever-pitch of excitement that by the time he entered her with such magnificent power she climaxed immediately, and tears slid down her cheeks as her body contracted sweetly and helplessly around him.

He must have tasted her tears, for he stopped that delectable thrusting and gathered her in his arms, soothing her and comforting her. 'I'm sorry,' he said into her hair.

She felt an unbearable sorrow scoring jagged fingers over her; she didn't know why—she didn't think she wanted to. 'What for?' she whispered.

'For always wanting to punish you,' he said, a strangely sad note in his own voice, too, and Kimberley's heart cried out for the love which eluded them, and she put her arms tightly around him.

'I can think of a lot worse kinds of punishment,' she whispered as he began to move again, taking her with him on another incredible but unbearably poignant journey into paradise.

Afterwards, he heard her sigh against his shoulder.

'What is it?'

'You make me feel——'

'What?'

She knew that she could only hint at the depths of the feelings he evoked in her. 'So—helpless, when you make love to me.'

'Do you think that I don't know?' he demanded, and his voice was savage. 'That it isn't the same for me, too?'

They slept then, exhausted, and when she awoke, some time in the night, Harrison had gone.

Things were very different between them after that. Better, but not perfect.

To the outside world they must have presented a united family front. When Harrison came home from work he played with the baby. Then, after she'd been bathed and fed, he and Kimberley would eat dinner together. At weekends, if it was fine, they took her to zoos and parks, even though she was much too young to appreciate it. On wet days they explored museums.

And at night Harrison made exquisite love to Kimberley in her big double bed. But he was never beside her in the morning.

And he remained an enigma to her; still she had no idea how that razor-sharp mind of his worked.

She had imagined—foolishly, perhaps—that the intimacies they shared every night might have brought them closer together, but the tenderness she unaskingly sought still eluded her.

In fact, she thought bitterly, waking one morning to find the rumpled sheets and her tender, bruised breasts and lips the only indication that Harrison had been there last night, making love with him seemed to have had the opposite effect from the one she'd wanted. If anything, Harrison seemed as distant as ever he'd been. If anyone had told her, years ago, that she would have been able to tolerate such a marriage she would have laughed in their faces.

But, amazingly, it was enough for her, and she counted her blessings rather than focus on the fact that what she wanted from Harrison was impossible, that he would never love her as she loved him.

But she had Georgia—she was blissfully happy in her role of mother. And if she couldn't have as much of Harrison as she wanted, well, she would just enjoy what she *did* have.

Until one night, when her world threatened to come crashing around her ears.

Harrison had just returned from Paris after a few days, and Kimberley had missed him unbearably.

Both picked without appetite at their supper, and when they went to bed—much earlier than usual—she was so eager and so hungry for him that she almost tore the clothes from his body, and he seemed to catch alight from her passionate fire immediately. They had never made love like it before.

It surpassed every other time—and Kimberley hadn't thought that was possible.

Afterwards, she was reluctant to let him go. Often he made love to her again, straight away, and then he would leave—go back to his own room, leaving her alone and bereft. She'd never asked him why, because she didn't want to hear his answer; deep in her heart she suspected that Harrison was one of those men who considered sleeping together all too intimate, too constricting.

But this time, as he made to pull himself out of her arms, she shook her head.

'Stay,' she murmured sleepily, her voice still slurred with pleasure.

She had wanted the closeness of falling asleep in each other's arms, but to her consternation he had obviously thought she'd meant one thing and one thing only, and he started to make love to her again.

Quickly her doubts were vanquished as the familiar feeling began to seep its way into her body. His hands worked their usual magic, and his kisses elicited a soft trembling which shivered down her body.

Then, just before he entered her, he said the most extraordinary thing. 'Pretend something for me, Kimberley.'

He was an imaginative lover, and she naturally assumed that he wanted her to enact some fantasy for him. 'Anything,' she murmured, her lips at his neck, revelling in the sweet taste of him. 'Anything you want.'

There was a pause. Then, in the oddest voice, he said, 'Pretend that you love me, just for tonight.'

Kimberley stiffened in horror.

What kind of game was he playing with her? Had he guessed? And was he going to torment her with the knowledge that he had known all along of the humiliating inequality in their relationship?

He released her from his embrace contemptuously, and, even though she could see that he was still helplessly aroused, he moved away from her, sat on the side of the bed and began pulling his jeans back on.

'I want a divorce,' he said abruptly, and Kimberley almost fainted. She had known that her love for him would be treated with scorn, but she hadn't dreamed that it would provoke such utter revulsion.

'What?' she whispered, in a hollow voice.

'You heard me. I want a divorce.' He turned and saw her frowning face. 'Oh, don't worry. I'll be extremely generous.'

Kimberley felt her heart lurch. So Tania had been right all the time. She had said he would go back to her. What was it? Something about possession being nine-tenths of the law, and that he would fight for Georgia. 'But what about the baby?' she asked quickly. She saw his non-comprehending frown. 'Are you going to fight me for her?'

His eyes hardened in response. 'Oh, don't worry—I won't contest custody of Georgia. I won't try and take her away from you. I never meant to, anyway—that was all an elaborate ploy.'

Now he wasn't making sense. What elaborate ploy?

'But I will want reasonable access,' he continued.

Kimberley nodded like an automaton. 'Of course,' she said stiffly, as though her heart weren't shattering into a million tiny pieces. She had to know. 'Is there someone else?' she asked, amazed that she could sound so cool at a moment like this.

'What?'

'That you want—to—to marry?' Not quite so cool now.

He made an impatient little noise. 'No, Kimberley, there's no one else.'

'Then——' She swallowed as he frowned. 'Would you mind telling me why?'

He stared at her as though she had just done something as fundamentally stupid as putting her hand in a fire. 'Twisting the knife, are you?' he enquired sardonically, and then he shook his head in resignation, spoke almost as if to himself. 'Oh, why not? Perhaps you deserve your moment of triumph.'

Moment of triumph? What on earth was he going *on* about? Kimberley was now even more confused, and in a way she was grateful for it, because her churned and puzzled thoughts were preventing her from taking in the unthinkable. That Harrison wanted a divorce.

'I want a divorce,' he said slowly, as if recognising some great truth, 'because I can no longer tolerate living in this kind of marriage.'

Kimberley stared at him, her eyes blank. Of course. 'Oh. I see.'

'I thought that it would work. I hoped... Oh, what the hell! There isn't any use in raking it all up again.'

She tried to be adult—brave. To retain what little dignity she had left. 'I do understand—honestly, I do. I think . . .' She hesitated painfully. 'That there has to be love for it to really work.'

He gave her a cold, empty smile. 'Exactly.' And he walked out of the room.

She lay in miserable silence for a time, almost relieved when she heard Georgia cry; at least feeding the baby would take her mind off things.

She fed the baby and changed her, and was just going back to her bedroom when she heard the sound of drawers being opened and slammed closed in Harrison's room. She pushed the door open and looked in, to find that he was throwing clothes haphazardly into a suitcase.

She met his hot, dark look of rage.

'Get out!' he snarled.

'What are you doing?'

'What does it look like?'

'Where are you going? You've only just got back.'

'I'm going,' he ground out, 'to a hotel. If you'd leave me in peace to do my packing.'

'You don't have to go to a hotel.'

'Yes, damn you—I do!'

'But I can take Georgia back to my house tomorrow——' she began, then stopped when she saw the look of black fury on his face.

'And doesn't it occur to you, you heartless little bitch, that it might be traumatic for me to live here once you've gone?'

He meant, of course, without Georgia. 'You'll have to get used to it,' she said, but it hit her hard to think how much he'd miss the baby he adored.

'Skip the patronising!' he gritted. 'And get out! If I want to stay in a hotel I don't need your permission to do it!'

And every adult and reasonable feeling she'd had died a sudden death as white-hot jealousy hit her like a sledgehammer. 'Why?' she taunted. 'So that you can meet Tania there? Tonight?'

His face, angry before, became positively murderous. 'Do you really think that I'm just going to leap straight from your bed and into Tania's arms?' he demanded.

'Well, you certainly couldn't wait to leap out of my bed night after night, that's for sure!' she said. 'So why shouldn't I think that?'

'Because I'm not interested in Tania—I never have been!'

'That's not what she thinks!'

'Tania's muddled thought-processes are really not my concern,' he said, in a bored, tired tone. 'Or yours. So why don't you do us all a favour, Kimberley, and go back to your own room?'

'You arrogant, horrible, hateful bastard!' she screamed at him. She flew at him, grabbing him by the arms, shocked at how hard and unforgiving the clenched muscles felt beneath her hands.

He didn't move, or react, just stood there with a contemptuous look all over his beautiful, arrogantly handsome face. 'I thought we'd agreed about being honest with one another? If it's sex you're after, Kimberley, then you only have to ask——'

And she burst into floods of tears, ran out and down the corridor, flinging herself on the bed and soaking her pillow within seconds.

'I'm sorry,' came a heavy voice from the doorway.

'Go away!'

'I seem to spend my whole time being foul to you...'

'So—so why do you do it?' she sobbed helplessly.

'You know why.'

'No, I don't.'

'Because we always hurt the ones we love,' he said bitterly, and Kimberley's tear-drenched eyes snapped open and she sat up, staring at him scornfully.

'Don't ever say that to me, Harrison,' she said quietly. 'Insult me if you have to, or hurt me—but never tell me lies. Not about that.'

He gave an ironic laugh. 'Oh, how I wish it were a lie, Kimberley. How uncomplicated my life would have been if I'd never had the misfortune to fall in love with you.'

Her eyes widened to kitten-like proportions. 'What are you talking about?' she said, in a strangled whisper.

'I was doomed,' he said, his mouth twisting with the memory, 'the moment I saw you.' A strange, frightening light flared from the depths of the cold grey eyes. 'How do you think it felt for a man to look on the woman his brother was going to marry and to want her for his own?'

'What?'

'Oh, I tried to fight it,' he said bitterly. 'And I managed for about ten seconds. And then I kissed you.'

Colour flooded her pale cheeks as she remembered the passion and the fervour, still so vivid, even after all this time.

'When you responded the way you did, an ugly, jealous and possessive streak sprang to life in me. I couldn't bear to think of you kissing other men like that—my *brother* like that.'

The torment on his face was indescribable. 'But I never kissed anyone like that,' she said. 'Except you.'

He nodded. 'Oh, yes, I realise that now. The trouble is that it has taken some time for me to understand and accept that what happens between us physically, while being very rare and quite amazing, has nothing to do with love—at least, not on your part.'

This really was fascinating. And very promising. Kimberley held her breath, surreptitiously pinched her wrist. Still there.

'I couldn't let you marry him. When I offered you the money and you accepted it, I felt both defeated and elated. My worst fears were realised— the woman I'd fallen in love with was nothing but a mercenary little tramp—but oh, some day, some day I would make her mine.'

Charming! She thought that he looked as though he was about to stop talking. 'Go on,' she urged.

He gave a humourless laugh. 'Why not? As I said earlier, perhaps you deserve to hear the truth. Where was I?'

'You were——' she found the glorious words ridiculously difficult to say, '—going to make me yours.'

'Yes.' Then he spoilt it completely by adding, 'Oh, I convinced myself that it was just your body I was after.'

Great!

'And I couldn't have you until Duncan had found someone of his own, of course. I didn't want to hurt my brother any more than I could. And I was right about that, as I'd known all along that I would be—Caroline is far more suited to him than you ever would have been.

'I'd planned to come to London to find you, after I'd been to Woolton, when fate played right into my hands with your mother's injured ankle. And then I saw you again, incongruously scrubbing a floor at Brockbank, that black hair spilling all the way down your back, those blue eyes lit with ice-fire, and I knew then that I'd been deceiving myself all along. That I wanted so much more than just your body. I wanted everything.

'The engagement party was my idea. Duncan and Caroline agreed, and it seemed the only way I could entice you anywhere near a social function that *I* would be attending. I'd planned to woo you, to court you. I certainly hadn't planned to take you to straight off to bed...' His voice tailed off in self-recrimination. 'But when I did I thought that I'd found paradise—only to wake up to find you getting dressed, about to creep away without a word, with a look of such distaste on your face that seemed to sum up exactly how you felt about what had happened.'

Kimberley blinked. Had the dream not *come* true—but been reality all along?

'Harrison,' she said softly.

He glared. 'What?'

'I love you.'

He froze, his eyes unmoving as they stared into hers.

'The reason I had such a look of disgust on my face after our night together was that I felt slightly appalled that in my virginal state I had enjoyed having my clothes literally torn off me. I wasn't sure that you'd respect me for that.'

His eyebrows disappeared completely into the thick abundance of his dark hair. 'Not respect you?' he murmured. 'You were every damned fantasy I'd ever had, come startlingly true.' His eyes narrowed. 'Will you please repeat what I thought you said a moment ago?'

She smiled, the happiness beginning to well up inside her. 'I love you, you stupid man—I've always loved you! And I'd have told you a darned sight sooner if you hadn't given such a good impression of seeming to loathe me.'

Was it something in her eyes, or in her voice, or in what she said which really convinced him? She never found out. But she knew the exact moment that he believed her, because he gave a slow, slow smile. 'Loathe you?' he echoed, on a groan. '*Loathe* you? Oh, my darling, darling Kimberley.'

And he moved and so did she, and they were in each other's arms, kissing, hugging, speaking only in half-sentences, all of which began with 'darling' or 'sweetheart'.

They ended up lying in each other's arms, staring into each other's eyes and hugging each other tightly, as if they could never bear to let each other go.

'Why else do you think I accepted your wretched money?' she demanded. 'Because I thought you hated me, and I knew how much I loved you. I thought that if I was only a mercenary little gold-digger in your eyes you'd never want to see me again!'

'That would,' he said wryly, 'be rather like reaching the summit of Mount Everest and not feeling proud of it!'

'You should write that down!' said Kimberley admiringly.

'You are also,' he said, 'the only woman who could make me so wild for her that all thoughts of contraception just flew out of the window.'

'Not even Tania?' said Kimberley nastily.

He moved to lie on top of her, and the sensation of that hard, lean body sent her senses singing. 'Listen to me,' he said, very gravely. 'My affair with Tania is all in her head.'

'Don't say you couldn't have had an affair with her?'

'Of course I could. I could have had affairs with lots of women. The whole point is that I didn't want to.'

Her eyes narrowed. 'Not at all?'

'Not once. Once I'd seen you . . . I'm afraid that was it.'

'And if I hadn't had Georgia——?'

'I would still have coerced you into marrying me.'

'And just how would you have gone about that?'

'Oh, I'd have thought of a way, don't worry,' he said with infuriating confidence. 'I was so convinced that we were twin souls, you see. And I was right.'

'Are you always so sure that you're right?' she queried dreamily.

'Mostly. But I thought that I could happily live with you, even if you didn't love me. In that I was hopelessly, hopelessly wrong. I vowed that I'd never spend the night with you until you told me you loved me.'

'Tonight's the night, then,' she murmured, her eyes sparkling with anticipation, but then she grew serious, shivered. 'How close we came to losing it all,' she whispered.

'Don't.' And he kissed her with a tender passion she had only ever dreamed of.

Soon he would make love to her again, and this time neither of them would need to hold anything back, but for the moment she was happy to be held, revelling in the closeness they now shared.

The joy of what lay before them was almost too frightening to contemplate, and they grinned at each other.

'I love you,' they both whispered, at exactly the same moment.

Now, that's *harmony*, thought Kimberley in delight, as she gave herself up ecstatically to his kiss.

Coming Next Month

HARLEQUIN PRESENTS®

Love can conquer the deadliest for

Indulge in Charlotte Lamb's seven-part series

#1822 DEADLY RIVALS
by Charlotte Lamb

Olivia realized that, to Max Agathios, she was merely the
trophy he had won from his deadly rival. Max wanted to
make war, not love!

Available in July wherever Harlequin books are sold.

SINS2

BRIDE'S
BAY RESORT

UNLOCK THE DOOR TO GREAT ROMANCE AT BRIDE'S BAY RESORT

Join Harlequin's new across-the-lines series, set in an exclusive hotel on an island off the coast of South Carolina.

Seven of your favorite authors will bring you exciting stories about fascinating heroes and heroines discovering love at Bride's Bay Resort.

Look for these fabulous stories coming to a store near you beginning in January 1996.

Harlequin American Romance #613 in January
Matchmaking Baby by Cathy Gillen Thacker

Harlequin Presents #1794 in February
Indiscretions by Robyn Donald

Harlequin Intrigue #362 in March
Love and Lies by Dawn Stewardson

Harlequin Romance #3404 in April
Make Believe Engagement by Day Leclaire

Harlequin Temptation #588 in May
Stranger in the Night by Roseanne Williams

Harlequin Superromance #695 in June
Married to a Stranger by Connie Bennett

Harlequin Historicals #324 in July
Dulcie's Gift by Ruth Langan

Visit Bride's Bay Resort each month wherever
Harlequin books are sold.

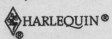

HARLEQUIN ®

BBAYG